Death By Lotto
A Josiah Reynolds Mystery

Abigail Keam

Worker Bee Press

Death By Lotto

Worker Bee Press
P.O. Box 485
Nicholasville, KY 40340

Abigail Keam

Acknowledgements

The author wishes to thank Al's Bar, which consented to be used as a drinking hole for my poetry-writing cop, Kelly, and Morris Book Shop. www.morrisbookshop.com

Thanks to my editor, Patti DeYoung.

Thanks to the Lexington Farmers' Market, www.lexingtonfarmersmarket.com

Artwork by Cricket Press
www.cricket-press.com

Book jacket by Peter Keam
Author's photograph by Peter Keam

By The Same Author

Death By A HoneyBee I
Death By Drowning II
Death By Bridle III
Death By Bourbon IV
Death By Lotto V
Death By Chocolate VI
Death By Haunting VII
Death By Derby VIII

The Princess Maura Fantasy Series

Wall Of Doom I
Wall Of Peril II
Wall Of Glory III
Wall Of Conquest IV

Last Chance For Love Romance Series

Last Chance Motel I
Gasping For Air II
The Siren's Call III

Audio Books

Last Chance Motel I
Gasping For Air II

Short Stories

Bobby Bobo Got Baptized At The Big Bone Baptist Church

To my parents, Arthur and Louise,
who sacrificed for me
and taught me to love reading.

Prologue

Ethel Bradley had fallen asleep in front of a flickering TV.

It was too bad.

If she had been awake, she might have discovered that she had won the lotto jackpot. The numbers that she played every week for over seventeen years–the birthdays of her deceased husband and son–had finally come in.

The lotto ticket was safely tucked inside her chubby little fist, which rested upon her heaving lap.

A younger hand gently reached over and pulled the ticket from her tiny hand while the announcer re-read the numbers.

Stunned at winning, the owner of the younger hand returned the ticket to Ethel's lap.

This would have to be handled with care. With a little finesse, this could play into a really big score, but would have to be thought through very carefully.

But one thing was for sure. There was no way Ethel Bradley was going to enjoy one dollar from that winning lotto ticket.

No damned way in hell!

1

Since no one knew I was coming home from New York, I hailed a cab at the Bluegrass Airport, a little jewel among airports. It was clean and efficient. One could park her car and be at her gate within ten minutes. How many airports could boast that? But this story is not about an airport or even an airline ticket.

It's about a lottery ticket.

My name is Josiah Reynolds. I was named after a Hebrew king because he was a righteous man before the Lord. My grandmother was a religious woman who thought that the meaning of that moniker might stick to me. It did not.

I'm a sinner.

Oh, I'm not an ax murderer. I don't kick puppies or push old ladies in front of buses. But I lie . . . frequently. It's becoming a bad habit and I've done things of which I'm not necessarily proud. I guess I'll have to have a long talk with God one of these days, but not right now.

All I could think about was that I would be home in twenty minutes and . . . within a half-hour I would feel better. I just had to get to my closet and into my secret stash.

Home is the Butterfly–a home built in the '80s that was to be a "cradle to the grave" house and at the cutting edge of design. The entire property was to be completely self-sufficient. It was made of local materials such as Kentucky limestone, timber and what locals call river marble. The entire back of the house is glass, which overlooks the Kentucky River.

It is called the Butterfly due to its second roof, which looks like wings from a distance. The roof's function was and still is to catch rainwater for underground cisterns that feed the pool and household needs. It also creates a dramatic waterfall in front of the house.

The Butterfly was one of the first "green" houses designed. My late husband built it for me and took credit for its design. It made him a star, except now he is dead. Died from a heart attack.

Back to me. I was cutting it very close. The color had drained from my face and I was sweating. It felt hot in the cab, but I knew the cab's heat wasn't the problem. Patting my face with an embroidered linen handkerchief, I tried to keep calm. Still, I didn't want to believe the entire fault was mine that I was in such a quandary.

"Can you go faster?" I asked the cab driver. My left hand began to twitch.

"Like to keep it around forty," mouthed the cabbie. "Road is awful curvy."

"What? What did you say?" The battery was going out on my hearing aid. Taking it from my ear, I shook it before putting it back. That helped a little.

Feeling the sweat break out on my forehead, I knew there was nothing I could do but endure my frustration. Looking out the window, I bit my lip, trying to control anticipated shakes.

Still, it was nice to see remnants of fall color along Tates Creek Road as we sped along the twisting black ribbon of country road. Trying to enjoy the sight of the Thoroughbreds in the fields, I sat uneasily in the back seat until we came to my driveway.

"Stop!" I commanded as soon as we pulled onto the gravel road.

I had the cab driver back up to the entrance where stood a huge sign with silver streamers stating "The Morgan Wedding."

The elderly driver asked, "Something wrong, honey?"

I scratched my chin like a perplexed chimp. "I'm not sure. It seems that someone is having a wedding at my place."

"Aw, ain't that nice," commented the cab driver, not realizing my increasing anxiety. "Let's go see?"

I felt an awful sensation in my gut. The last wedding I had been to ended up in a murder/suicide during the "I do's." I was not ready to repeat the experience. But at least it had not been at my house. Who were the Morgans and what were they doing on my farm?

"Go easy now. The road has dips," I cautioned. Holding tight to the door handle, I scanned for changes. My rescue racehorses were in the front field like always. Various peacocks, sheep, and geese had to be coaxed from the road with the cab's horn onto the grassy shoulder . . . like always.

Matt's little bungalow looked the same as we passed. I noted that his car was in the driveway. That was good. He was home. I relaxed a little bit.

But as we drove closer to the Butterfly, I could see festivities of some kind were indeed taking place.

A young man ran toward the cab and opened my door.

"Who are you?" I blurted out, peering around his coltish frame.

"Huh?" he asked in a dull tone. No bright spark behind those unblinking brown eyes.

I repeated, "Who are you?"

Looking confused, he poked his head in the cab, "I'm the parking valet. Are you getting out or what?"

"What's going on here?" I demanded, my fingers nervously tapping my bad leg.

The young man looked at the cab driver for help. Glancing in the front mirror, she returned a disgruntled shrug. "Picked her up at the airport."

Suddenly the front cab door opened and in popped Mrs. Eunice Leticia Todd, my part-time housekeeper and mother to Shaneika Mary Todd, my criminal lawyer.

Wondering why I need a criminal lawyer? You must be from out-of-town or don't read the paper. Let's just say that I seem to be a beacon for all the crazies in the Bluegrass.

The first story started over a year ago, when Richard Pidgeon was found dead in one of my beehives. The primary detective on the case—a Fred O'nan—had been one of my students when I taught art history at the University of Kentucky. I turned him in when he was caught cheating on an exam, causing him to lose his baseball scholarship as a result. Seeing this as an opportunity to get back at me, he made my life a living hell until I had him thrown off the case, giving him a bad mark on his record. That's when he flipped his lid and tried to kill me by pulling us both off a cliff.

Since then there have been other people trying to do me harm, but I've beaten both the police and the grim reaper. That is . . . so far.

"My goodness," Mrs. Todd exhaled, obviously annoyed. "What are you doing home? Honey, drive around and go back to that little green house that you passed on the way in. Thank you." She waved the parking valet away and settled in the front seat, turning around to face me.

"What's going on, Eunice?" I asked.

"You said that you were going to stay in New York for awhile," she hedged.

I disliked the accusing tone in her voice. "I got bored and decided to come home for the holidays. Now, what's going on?"

Eunice flashed a big smile. "I wanted to try it out before I talked to you about it, but you've caught me red-handed. I did get permission from Matt for a trial run."

I squeaked, "Try what out?"

"A way that the Butterfly could be utilized and we both could make some money." She held up her hand before I could speak. "Now, hear me out before cussing up a blue streak."

I noticed that the cab driver was driving very slowly. Even with my cane, I could have walked faster. Obviously she wanted to hear what Mrs. Todd had to say.

I gave them both a look of extreme displeasure. I was tired. My bad leg was throbbing and I was hungry. I hadn't eaten since yesterday. I just kept thinking that I needed to get into my house.

"We're both just wasting away with nothing to do. Your girl is living in London. My girl doesn't need me right now. But we both are bright and in reasonably good health. We can still contribute with the skills we have.

"Now what do we have? You've got a huge important house that everyone wants to see. I've got skills that are rusting away. I used to run a boutique hotel in Bermuda.

"I'm a good cook and know how to cater big functions. Now if I can please stuffy British aristocrats with money up the whazoo, excuse my vulgarity . . . and your fussy ways, I know I can serve the Bluegrass clientele. Why not put the two together and open up the Butterfly for special occasions like weddings?"

"Jumping Jehosaphat! Have strangers paw through my things? I should think not."

"Now all of that has been taken care of. The wing with your office and bedroom/bathroom has been sectioned off. No one can get into it."

"Oh my goodness, this is just terrible. What have you done to my house . . . my privacy? I feel like punching something, someone . . . like you, yeah you, in the face. I'm so mad. Let me out of the damn cab before I really hit someone."

The cab rolled to a stop right before Matt's little bungalow, which used to be the caretaker's shed.

Eunice's almond-shaped eyes widened. This was not going as planned and she needed to get back to the Butterfly.

Scrambling for money in my purse, I threw some bills at the cab driver. In a hurry to leave the cab, I couldn't get my door to stay open. I'd release it, pushing it open in my anger only to have it slam shut on me again. "Hells bells!" I screeched.

The screen door to the house opened and out stepped Matt with Baby, my 225-pound English Mastiff. Upon seeing me, Baby bounded down the steps and reared up on the back cab door, barking. With his good eye, he peered through the window, now smudged with his drool.

Now I really couldn't get out.

One thing about Baby: I always tried to be the decent human he expected me to be, so I calmed down. I didn't want Baby to witness me being a jerk.

Matt pushed Baby off the vehicle and pulled open the back cab door while Baby deliriously chased his tail in happiness.

Eunice Todd stepped out as well, standing a little behind Matt.

The cab driver also got out and took my bags from the rear. She wasn't upset at all as she now had a delicious story to tell her coworkers about how Josiah Reynolds flipped out. I was well known in town.

So now everyone was out of the cab, but me.

Matt extended his hand, which I grabbed. He basically wrenched me from the back seat.

"What's going on at my house, Matt?" I accused. "You were supposed to watch things for me."

"I have," replied Matt with a crooked smile.

I just wanted to slap that sneer off his gorgeous face. Did I mention he looked like the matinee idol, Victor Mature, a big movie star from the '40s and '50s, who was a homeboy from Louisville? Mature was known for his wit and was quoted as saying, "Hollywood is a place where the stars twinkle until they wrinkle."

Okay, that quote was not on the Oscar Wilde or Noel

Coward level of wit, but it still brought a smile to my face.

Here's a little known movie fact: *The Maltese Falcon,* directed by John Huston, is considered the first American film noir movie. However, it is *I Wake Up Screaming* with Victor Mature and Betty Grable—you know Betty, the girl with the million-dollar gams during WWII and favorite pinup girl of "the greatest generation" red-blooded males. However, *I Wake Up Screaming* was not released until after *The Maltese Falcon*—so it loses its place in film history.

Film noir is French for black film, which characterizes stylized black and white movies dealing with urban crime from the '40s and '50s. This type of cinematography was named by the French critic, Nino Frank; however, the look of these films comes from German expressionist directors who fled Hitler's Germany. Just thought you should know. These things are important if you want to know me. I'm crazy about film noir, but I digress.

"How do you explain strangers in my house then?"

Matt asked, "Miss Eunice, do you need to get back?"

She glanced hesitantly at me and then at Matt. "I think the bride and groom are about to cut the cake."

Matt grabbed my arm before I could gesture something rude. "I'll take care of this. You go on back and take care of the guests. Don't worry about Josiah. After a mint julep and some food, she'll be fine. I expect that her blood sugar is low. Go on now."

I tried to jerk my arm from Matt's iron grip but couldn't. I hated it when he treated me like a naughty child.

"If you say so. I'll take the cab back to the house," she replied, before giving one last awkward glance at the both of us.

I knew all too well what she saw.

A slightly crumpled, bewildered-looking woman with a huge dog with his snout now stuck up her crotch while held captive by a much taller GQ poster boy in immaculate khakis and a Ralph Lauren Egyptian white cotton shirt.

Looking relieved she jumped back in the cab and rolled up her window so she wouldn't have any final communication with me. To my total embarrassment, Eunice was laughing. I know she was. Her shoulders were shaking.

As the cab pulled away, I jerked away from Matt and pushed Baby away from my "personal life." "Do you mind?" I scolded Baby.

In response, Baby licked my hand, depositing a nice layer of slime.

Sighing, I muttered, "Some things never change." Still, I was relieved that my dog was happy to see me. I rubbed his floppy ears and kissed the scar running down from his massive forehead to his bad eye. He received these injuries as a puppy while trying to protect me from that crazy cop, Fred O'nan. How could I not love him?

"This is not the dignified return home of a conquering heroine," I complained.

Matt acted as though he didn't hear as he picked up my luggage and strode into his little cottage. The screen door slammed. The sound made me flinch. It had sounded like a gunshot.

I limped up the five steps to his porch and stepped inside his tasteful abode of bachelor comforts complete with a big screen TV and large pieces of lounging furniture–all in various colors of browns and tans, of course.

If Matt wanted to really be wild, he purchased something in navy.

Strolling back from the guest bedroom where he had placed my luggage, Matt beckoned to his couch.

"Leg hurt?"

"Like a bitch."

Matt arched a black eyebrow. "I see that we have developed a potty mouth while in New York. You've cussed more in five minutes than I usually hear in a year."

I slumped down on the couch. Matt joined me and brought my legs up to his lap. Carefully, he took off my shoes and began rubbing my feet. I cooed as I nestled into big comfy pillows.

"Your left foot is hot. No wonder you're in a bad mood. How much pain are you in?" He kept rubbing while looking expectantly at me. Matt knew something was not right.

I was acting weird, even for me.

"Careful," I cautioned. "The skin is really tender there."

Matt readjusted my leg.

"That's why I came home. For some reason, my pain

level has shot up and I've run out of pain medication."

"Why didn't you have a doctor in New York give you a prescription?"

"I tried, but she called my doctor down here and was told that I wasn't due for a refill until next month."

"You've gone through everything?"

"I had to double the dose. My leg hurts like the dickens. Something's out of kilter."

"You're right. Your skin is hot on the left foot, but not on the right."

"Matt. I'm completely out. I've got to get inside my house. I have some . . . extra . . . medication there."

"No problem. Tell me where it is and I'll get for you."

I bit my lip. "Well, that's going to be a problem. You see, it's a little stash that Asa left for me in case of emergencies."

Matt's eyes rolled in the back of his head. "Christ, you're talking about illegal pain killers."

"Please, Matt. Get me the medication. It was all I could do to keep it together on the plane. Please, Matt. I'm begging."

"Josiah, I say this with complete love and affection. If the doctor doesn't find anything wrong with you, and you still need all this high-powered pain medication–then, my little dove, you're going into rehab."

"Matt, please. No lectures now. Please. Please. I'm in pain. The pills are in a floor safe in my clothes closet. Get me a pencil. I'll write down the numbers."

I finally had to tell Matt the combination, as my hand

shook so badly that I couldn't write. He called Eunice and gave her some lame story that I needed something and he had to get into my bedroom.

She unlocked the side door for him and Matt slipped in unnoticed by the wedding party. Shutting the closet door, he found the safe, which he opened on the first go around.

He pulled out some big nasty-looking pills plus two maryjane ciggies. But before he closed the safe, he discovered important-looking papers and gave them a thorough perusal before putting them back. Giving the closet one last check, Matt closed it and then met Eunice by the side door.

She gave him a large basket of food from the wedding.

Matt gave her a quick peck on the cheek before sliding out the side door and racing to his bungalow.

By that time, I was crying from the pain.

Matt took one look at my tear-stained face and crumbled. "Hold on, Rennie. You're going to feel better in a few minutes. I'm gonna fix you a hot plate of food and get some medication inside you." He thrust a lit marijuana cigarette at me. "Here. Smoke this in the meantime."

I knew by taking such chances as giving me illegal medication, Matt could lose his license to practice law and could go to jail. I was putting both Matt and my daughter, Asa, in terrible positions. Still, I gratefully took the joint, inhaling its musty smoke.

Rennie was Matt's pet name for me, after the actor Michael Rennie.

Matt had met me at a party where I whispered Michael Rennie's commands to the robot, Gort, from the movie, *The Day The Earth Stood Still* in his ear for a bet.

Matt had won and we had been friends ever since.

After pouring a large sweet iced tea for me, Matt put a plate together and put it on a TV tray. I was famished.

"I crushed up some pills and mixed them in the mashed yams."

I was grateful that Matt had already cut the chicken into small pieces. I still struggled with knives.

I took a couple of bites of the mashed yams and finished my iced tea. I started to take another bite, but my hands started to feel really heavy and my eyelids fluttered. "Matt!" I cried. "I feel fun . . . ."

2

The next morning I woke up feeling dizzy. I cradled my head until I realized that my leg wasn't throbbing. I tried to think. The last thing I remembered was that I was trying to tell Matt that I felt sleepy. It took me a few moments to recognize that I was in Matt's guest room at his bungalow.

Slowly I got out of bed. On a chair was placed an outfit that I could get into easily, complete with fresh undies. Leaning against the chair was my ebony cane with the silver wolf's head.

I wondered what Matt thought when he saw the cane, since Franklin had purchased it in Key West. Did he think of Franklin at all? Did he think he had made a mistake when he cut Franklin loose? He never talked about it.

At least not to me.

Anyway, Franklin was Matt's boyfriend, whom Matt dumped so he could marry Meriah Caldwell, the famous mystery writer. They got down to the "I do's" in the church when Lacey Bridges shot a wedding guest during the ceremony . . . right in front of me. Then Lacey put the gun in her mouth . . . you can imagine the rest. It was quite a shock and put a stop to the wedding, and finally, the relationship.

I love Matt, but I don't understand him.

Finally presentable, I limped into the living room. Mrs. Todd was making breakfast. I gave her a feeble wave.

Eunice asked, "Do you feel better, honey?"

"I feel like someone slipped me a Mickey last night."

"Matt told me that he put sleeping medication in your food so you would get a good night's rest."

"Ahh, that explains it–but I do feel better."

"Good. Good. Matt said to keep an eye on you until you got settled in the Butterfly. Now you sit down at the table. I've got some nice pecan pancakes ready to grill."

"Bacon? Not too crisp."

"Coming right up. A good breakfast will set you right up and when you get ready, we can have our talk."

"Has the bridal party left?"

"Over an hour ago. They're at their bridal breakfast right now."

"Goodness. They've pulled out all the stops. A breakfast. Where?"

"Over at Lady Elsmere's house. Lady Elsmere let us use all her antique china and silver. I must say the table looked splendid. It was a small party of thirty, so we could still use her dining room table. It took a while, though, to find all of the leaves to it."

I took a drink of my tomato juice, wishing a little vodka had been tossed in. You know–a little eye-opener in the morning. "Is Charles okay with this extra work?"

Eunice flipped the pancakes over while the bacon sizzled. "Charles isn't in charge of the house anymore."

"What?"

"Lady Elsmere told him he had to start running the farm and overseeing the horses since he was going to be inheriting the property. He's moved into the Big House and, instead of serving dinner, he sits with Lady Elsmere now."

Eunice placed a plate of golden brown pancakes topped with melting butter cradled by gobs of bacon on the table.

Before I could ask for the maple syrup, she placed a warmed glass bottle of Kentucky maple syrup before me. After going back to the stove, she returned with a bowl of grits.

I poured the expensive syrup over my pancakes and took a bite. Yum. I was in heaven.

Most people don't associate Kentucky with maple syrup, but many farmers tap the sugar maple tree and cook the sap down until the liquid is a buttery golden color. It's expensive because it is labor intensive, but the product is worth it since it is not mixed with corn syrup like grocery brands are.

I don't believe in buying cheap corn-based food. Pay the man what his product is worth is what I always say.

I will buy a $15 free-range chicken from the Farmers' Market. I will pay that much because I know that the chicken has had a good natural life until harvested.

From that expensive chicken, I can make several meals. The chicken will cook in my crock-pot until it falls apart. With the broth and dark meat, I will make a homemade noodle or rice soup with summer or fall vegetables.

With one breast, I will make a chicken/rice casserole with broccoli/squash, smothering it with local cheese, which I'll bake. The other piece of white meat is served with mashed potatoes or yams and a salad. The parts that I don't want will be mixed in Baby's food. (Always remember not to give your pets the bones. They are too soft.) So the expensive chicken turns out to be the base of seven or more meals for less than $2.00 each.

And I don't have to worry about inhumane treatment of the animal while alive, or antibiotics and other nasty stuff fed to it coming back to haunt me.

But I digress again. Let's get back to the story. "Who in charge of the house?"

"Lady Elsmere's grand-nephew by her late husband came to visit and he brought his man with him."

"Is the nephew still here?"

Eunice sat at the table with her plate of pancakes. Reaching for the syrup, she said, "Yes. And he's been making it his life's work to meet every rich widow in Kentucky."

"Hmmm," I replied before putting more butter on my cakes. "What does Charles think?"

"Charles thinks this nephew has his eye on the farm and has put his man in charge so he could report back to the nephew the goings-on."

"Is this the nephew who inherited Lord Elsmere's estate?"

Eunice swallowed and gently patted her mouth before speaking. "He is the man's brother."

"Do hush now!"

"Unhuh. See what I mean."

"I see the need for concern. This might be an adventurer planning to steal Charles' inheritance away from him."

"And since that new butler has taken over, Lady Elsmere keeps getting crankier and crankier with Charles. Things in the house are missing. Food is arriving at the table cold. The wine is not served correctly. I hear tell that she hates white wine being served warm which it has been lately."

"Why doesn't she put Charles back in charge?"

"Because the new man says it's Charles' fault. He accused Charles of trying to make him look bad. There was a big row at the house last week between the two. Mike Connor told Shaneika and she told me." She took a sip of her coffee. "Things have settled down some, but I think there's still tension."

"My goodness, I will have to go over there today and just stick my nose in Lady Elsmere's business," I announced with glee. "But let's get back to my house, okay."

Eunice Todd leaned over and pulled a folder out of her purse lying beside the table. "Look at this. It's a business plan for next year."

I opened the folder.

"And here is something else." Eunice pushed a check toward me.

"What's this?"

"Your portion of the proceeds."

I gave the check a glance. "Two thousand dollars?"

"And that's after everything has been paid. Pure profit."

"What's your cut?"

"The same."

I nodded my approval. Even with my settlement from the city, I was on a very conservative budget. Things were better since I had started boarding horses, but I was still on a tight leash. The money from the city paid for my medical expenses while the honey sales and the boarded horses paid for the farm expenses. I have very little money for my own personal use. The two hundred thousand Shaneika paid me for ten acres went to repair the Butterfly.

My only vain expenses were having my hair done, plus buying flower arrangements for the house. Of course, Baby was a small fortune, but I owed him.

I checked the date on the check from Eunice's personal account. "So this check is good to go?"

"The bridal party paid by visa, so the check is good. What do you think?"

"How many a year?"

"Let's start with ten and see what happens, but I think more than ten would be pushing it for me."

"And my personal items would be protected?"

"There is a walk-through before the bridal party leaves. If something is not right, I'll know about it. They have to check out with me or there is an automatic penalty fee."

"And they will always use the west wing?"

"If they stay overnight. Otherwise, only the general living areas will be used. The wing with your bedroom and office will be shut off. Nobody will be able to get in."

I thought for a moment, rubbing my finger around the juice glass rim. Two thousand dollars was tempting.

"What about the tours?"

"The tours will be cut back to one day a week. They just don't make as much money as a wedding." Eunice looked at me hopefully. "And if you don't mind me saying so, you should allow school groups to come out here. You're just letting the Butterfly go to waste. It should be full of people and goings-on."

"I have a crazy person trying to kill me. I think that accounts for the lock-down."

"He's under control. If he gets free, then we can rethink things, but until then—open this house up and let it breathe. You can't live your life in fear that O'nan might show up one day."

"I'm tempted, Eunice. I really could use the money, but I'd like to talk it over with my daughter first and then Matt."

Eunice patted my arm. "That's fine, honey. It's a step in the right direction. We're both still too young to be put out to pasture. You think about it and get back to me." She rose from the table and, seemingly satisfied with our conversation, started to wash the dishes. She hummed Sam Cooke's *You Send Me* while filling the sink with hot water.

I went to make my bed and gather my personal belongings. As soon as the kitchen was tidy, Eunice was going back to the Butterfly.

Baby helped make the bed by depositing little droplets of drool where he tried to smooth out the bedspread with his snout. Then he discovered a food stain, which he licked clean, leaving a huge wet spot on the bedspread.

Giving the room one final look, I declared it fit for the next guest and called for Baby to follow me. I didn't think one night's use required the sheets to be washed. Matt had been thoughtful enough to leave my electric golf cart at the bungalow. I dropped Eunice off at the Butterfly, and with Baby in tow, we headed for Lady Elsmere's house.

I usually entered through the kitchen since "my accident" as the steps to the portico were bothersome. Opening the back door, I walked into the mudroom that led into the kitchen where workers were busy peeling, boiling, paring, and smoking.

Smoking? Charles didn't allow smoking in the house unless it was a guest.

I didn't recognize any of the staff. Where was Charles' family who worked in the kitchen?

The workers turned and stared. One man approached me, and in a French accent, asked, "May I help you?"

Not recognizing the kitchen help either, Baby placed himself in front of me, growling slightly.

The Frenchman, holding a ladle, stepped back.

"He usually gets treats when he visits," I announced. "He won't bite."

"Qu'est-ce que c'est?"

I thought quickly, but my French was horrible. "Ummm, plisir, umm no, gaterie pour une chienne."

Undoubtedly the chef checked Baby out. Grinning, he said, "Non, Madame, chien."

"Oui, he's a male," I smiled while holding onto Baby's collar.

The French chef muttered something in French to one of his workers and a nice piece of flank steak appeared. He carefully placed the steak on newspaper and set it near us.

Baby looked up as if to ask permission.

"It's okay, Baby. Knock yourself out."

The French chef conveyed to his crew that my dog's name was Baby. "Bébé," laughed the Chef.

The crew looked at Baby and cheerfully called his name. "Hey Bébé. Bébé bonjour."

Another worker carefully placed a large bowl of water next to Baby and scooted away fast when Baby turned his face so his good eye could see who was near him.

"What in the Queen's name is going on?"

I turned to see a smallish man with reddish hair in an impeccably tailored suit.

All the workers scurried to their respective tasks and left me alone to tell the tale.

Thinking that he must be Lady Elsmere's great-nephew, I strode toward him and held out my hand. "Hello, I'm Josiah Reynolds, the next door neighbor."

The little man gave me a stony glare as if it pained him to speak to such an oaf. "I am Giles, Sir Anthony's manservant."

I hastily lowered my hand. Oooops! One does not shake hands with servants.

"Very nice to meet you, Giles. I'm going to visit June, I mean Lady Elsmere. Come, Baby."

Giles stepped toward me, blocking my way. He turned his head a little when he heard Baby's low growl coming from his left.

"You're in my way," I said curtly.

"Do you have an appointment with her Ladyship?"

"Uh, Giles, neighbors don't make appointments in Kentucky. We just drop by. It's called being neighborly."

"Her Ladyship is busy right now. Perhaps you can leave a card?"

I gave Giles a nasty smile. I so disliked men telling me what to do. "See this dog," I said. "This is a trained attack dog."

Baby cocked his head to one side and let his long tongue droop out the side of his mouth. He began panting.

"Stick with me," I mumbled to Baby. To Giles I demanded, "Now if you don't let me pass, I'm gonna give Baby the command to attack."

Giles looked with contempt at Baby. "I don't think that dog is capable of much except drooling puddles, which is what he's doing now on this antique, parqúet floor."

Seeing that I was not going to intimidate this little pug of a man, I just stepped around him and went down the hallway. After giving a huge sneeze, Baby followed suit.

In the foyer I met Amelia, Charles' daughter. We spoke briefly and after telling me that she was glad that I was back, she directed me to the breakfast room where June was having coffee with a friend.

"Hello," I announced, opening the breakfast room door.

"Darling," cooed Lady Elsmere, aka June Webster from Monkey's Eyebrow, Kentucky. "When did you get back?"

I kissed her cheek. "Yesterday."

"Why didn't you let anyone know you were coming home?" she asked, while eying Baby who had lain down in front of the doorway, as was his nature to do.

"It was sort of a last-minute thing."

June gave me the once-over, but decided her questioning could wait. "Josiah, this is my childhood friend, Ethel Bradley. We went to school together."

I reached forward to shake hands with Ethel who returned my smile.

"Such warm hands," she commented after releasing mine.

"Thank you." I didn't mention that her's were frigid. Pouring myself some hot tea, I laced it with honey from the honey pot and buttered some toast. Oh, there was jam too. My toast needed some jam as well. Any possibility of eggs? Maybe? Two breakfasts in one morning! Things were looking up.

Lady Elsmere asked, "Josiah, don't you ever eat breakfast at home?"

"I squeeze a grapefruit now and then." Why tell her the truth?

Just then there was a loud crash and commotion coming from the formal dining room.

"What now?" cried Lady Elsmere, exasperated. "Is that bloody wedding breakfast still going on?" She gave me an evil look. "I don't know how I was ever talked into renting my house. What will my friends think when they hear of it?"

"The same thing they said when you started giving tours of your farm."

"And what was that, Josiah?"

"That you're an astute business woman." I took a bite of toast. "Besides, it's for a good cause. Me."

"Hmmm. That so? I just hope they haven't broken something precious. Anyway, I'll deal with that later. It's portentous that you are here, Josiah," announced Lady Elsmere.

"Why's that?" I asked before biting again into my jam-slathered toast.

"Ethel has been concerned lately. Frankly, I told her to hire a detective, but now that you are here . . ."

"Whoa there. I just got back from New York yesterday. I'm in no shape to go gallivanting around the countryside. No offense, Miss Ethel."

"Just listen to Ethel. Perhaps you can give some advice on how to handle the matter."

"Oh, I see. Sorry about that. Yes, indeed. Miss Ethel, what seems to be the problem?"

Miss Ethel looked at me with watery blue eyes and although they seemed worn out, they conveyed a certain warmth . . . a kindness that some people possess. But then everything about Miss Ethel seemed worn out, from her frayed dress to her thinning blue-gray hair. While

June was the same age, she still possessed a certain regalness while Miss Ethel looked like an overly wrinkled prune–but a sweet prune.

Miss Ethel gave a shy look at June before turning to me. "Well, if you think so, June," she replied before collecting her thoughts on her problem.

After a moment of silence, I prodded, "Miss Ethel?"

"It's hard to put into words," she blurted. "So strange. So strange."

"Let's begin at the beginning, shall we?" I encouraged.

"Quite so. Yes. The beginning." She looked up at the ceiling. "The beginning."

"Just tell her what you told me, Ethel," urged Lady Elsmere.

Ethel fixed her weak blue eyes on me and began. "I hope you don't think that I'm daffy because I'm not, but I think someone is trying to kill me."

I asked, "What makes you think so?"

"Bizarre things have been happening. Things that have never happened before. Like this week, I had a car accident. I've never had an accident before in my life."

"You still drive?" I asked.

"Oh yes, or I would have no transportation, but my nephew, Jubal, sometimes drives me."

"I see. What makes you think this accident was questionable? Everyone has an accident sooner or later, no matter how good a driver she may be."

"My brakes went out, you see. Just plum out. I was lucky that I could safely coast into an old tobacco field."

"Unhuh," I murmured.

"The mechanic said the brake line looked like it had been cut!" Ethel scooted back triumphally in her chair. "See." She gave a curt nod.

Ethel now had my attention. "Anything before that?"

"Two things. I love apple cider and always purchase it from a local orchard. Now I have bought cider from this particular orchard for years and never had any problem. That same week, I took a drink out of a new bottle and got very ill. I had the worst stomach cramps."

"Was the bottle's seal intact?"

"I don't remember if it was or not."

"Did you complain to the orchard?"

"I called them and they said that the cider was made from a large batch and no one else had called about a problem. Only me."

"Did you have the cider tested?"

"My house cleaner poured it out, unintentionally of course. She just thought it was a bad batch."

"Anything else?"

"I would swear on the Bible that someone went through my house."

"Searched it?"

"Yes, my drawers looked different. I'm very neat, Mrs. Reynolds, and my drawers looked different." Ethel smiled. "Then the little knick-knacks in my curio seemed like they had been moved. Nothing big, just little things caught my eye."

"And when did this happen?"

"After I went to church on Sunday morning."

"When did the car accident occur?"

"Monday morning."

"Where do you live?"

"Outside Perryville in my husband's family home. We have . . . I mean I have about forty-five acres which I lease out. That provides a little extra income for me."

"How close are your neighbors?"

"Not too far around the bend in the road, but they wouldn't be able to see anything. Besides, the house sits back off the road."

"Do you have good relations with your neighbors?"

"Oh yes, for years. I don't think they have anything to do with this."

"Why is that?"

"Just something I feel . . . intuition."

"Do you have any home security systems in place?"

"No, but I have good sound locks."

"Did you find any doors or windows unlocked during those two days?"

"That's the strange thing. The house was locked up tight."

"Do you have an extra key under the mat or does anyone else have a key to the house?"

"Oooh, I would never leave an extra key under the mat. No. No. I do have an extra key, but it was in my car, which I had with me."

"Did you check to see if the key was still there?"

"I checked. It was and no one else has a key to my house. No one."

"Not even the bank, close friend or a relative?"

"No one."

I thought for a moment. "Does anyone know of the second key's existence or could someone have stolen your key and had a copy made?"

"I don't think so. No one knows of the second key as it is in the passenger seat where the fabric has torn a little bit. It's my little secret."

"What about friends or this Jubal getting the main key out of your handbag?"

Ethel gave a flustered sigh. "I just don't see that. I really don't."

"Where do you keep your handbag when you are home?"

Ethel gave Lady Elsmere a bewildered look.

"I told you Josiah would be thorough. If you want to find out what's happening, you have to go through the process of elimination, dear," coaxed Lady Elsmere. "Trust her. Josiah's smart. She's good at puzzles."

"I always keep my handbag on the kitchen table. I go out the back door to get into my car. The front door is always locked."

"I have a few more questions . . . if you will allow me."

"Go ahead, dear."

"Is there a separate key for the back door?"

"The key works on both locks."

"I see. Who was in your house before all this started happening?"

Ethel thought for a moment. "Well, my housekeeper. She comes once a week, but she has worked for me over fifteen years and is honest as the day is long. Then Jubal, that's my nephew, comes over often to check on me. He was there the week before I started noticing things."

"So two people. That's all?"

"Yes."

"No window washers or gas men? No deliveries?"

"I'm sure of it."

"Okay, we're getting somewhere. Was there anything different that you did that week, something out of character for you? Did you bump into someone in the grocery store you hadn't seen in a long time, or someone coming to the door asking questions? Anything different in your routine?"

"No, nothing." Ethel thought hard for a moment. "Well, the only thing that was different was that I asked Jubal to buy a lottery ticket for me. I didn't feel well that day, so he went."

My heart started beating faster. "Tell me about this."

"I know this sounds silly, but every week I buy a lottery ticket with my late husband and son's birthdays as the numbers. It is my way of honoring them. My husband died in a farming accident. The tractor turned over on him. And then my son died in Vietnam. Both silly tragedies." Her wrinkled cheeks became flushed as she looked at Lady Elsmere for support.

"It's not that I expect to win or that I even need the money. After all, I have my social security and my husband's pension. But I thought that if I did, I would give the money away to worthwhile causes in their names. It was my little way of honoring their lives, you see."

Lady Elsmere reached over and clasped her friend's hand. "That's a lovely sentiment, Ethel. Just lovely."

"Thank you."

"Did Jubal give you the ticket?"

"Of course."

"Did you win?"

Ethel gave a bitter little laugh. "No, I never win."

"Are you sure?"

"Yes, dear, I checked the paper on Sunday. I didn't win."

"What did you do with the ticket?"

"I always keep the tickets in my Bible to use as bookmarks."

"Does Jubal know where you keep the tickets? The housekeeper?"

"Yes to both."

"Was your Bible at home during the times that you thought someone was searching?"

Ethel's face seemed to come alive. "Now that you mentioned it, yes. I thought the Bible had been moved from its regular place on my night stand."

"How do you mean?"

"Well, I always place my Bible facing toward me on the nightstand, right on the edge, so it is easy for me to reach. The day that I thought someone had been in the house, the Bible was placed the same way, but too far away for me to reach easily when I was in bed. That's when I noticed the difference. I had to lean over to pick it up."

"Did your car accident happen after this?"

"Yes. Oh, goodness, you don't think my nephew had anything to do with it?"

"Is he a blood nephew?"

"No, he is my husband's brother's son."

"So he's really not any blood kin to you," I thought out loud.

"One never knows about nephews," said Lady Elsmere. "I've got one on my hands now whom I would like to chuck out. They can be a nuisance." She turned and looked at me. "What do you think?"

"I would hire a private investigator as you suggested, June. And I would stay with someone until this is over," I said to Ethel. "Plus, I would have a home security system installed with a camera at both doors so you can see if anyone goes in or out of your house when you're not there."

Ethel's eyes grew very wide. "Really? Oh dear, this sounds serious."

"I would take it seriously too. Take it from someone who didn't take things seriously enough and got thrown off a cliff for it. Better to err on the side of caution."

"That settles it. You'll stay with me, Ethel. I won't take no for an answer," demanded June.

"What about a change of clothes?"

I looked at Lady Elsmere. "Send Amelia over for a change of clothes."

"I have a cat, Petty."

"Amelia will feed Petty for you. It would only be for a few days until an investigator checks things out for you."

"Whom shall I hire? I hope they're not too expensive."

"I'll call a detective who's a friend of mine. He'll know of someone local who is reputable." I started to rise. "I just got back home. Haven't even checked on my bees yet, so you ladies must excuse me. I'll be in touch later."

"Oh, we have been an imposition," declared Ethel. She wrung her hands in concern.

Lady Elsmere laughed. "Don't worry, Ethel. Josiah loves to be in the middle of intrigue. She would've been angry if we hadn't confided in her."

I scrunched my nose at June. "See y'all later."

Not wanting to face Giles again, I went out through the breakfast room. I climbed in the golf cart, but not before I had to help Baby climb in. "Hey, who is disabled here, dog!" I leaned against the cart for a few minutes, breathing hard.

Baby gave me a look of satisfaction. I really don't think he needed help getting in. He just wanted attention.

Well, he wasn't the only one.

3

"From what you've told me, there's not much the police can do. She's not really sure that someone was in her house."

"She has a strong feeling that things have been moved," I said to Detective Goetz.

"Police don't move on feelings. They have to have proof. As for the car incident, I called Mrs. Bradley's mechanic and he said that the brake line could have possibly been cut by a rock."

"She doesn't have a history of being histrionic. I think Mrs. Bradley is correct in her assessment that something is not right."

Goetz took a bite of his mac and cheese casserole with broccoli that Eunice cooked for lunch from my recipe. He had sounded happy to hear from me when I called, and didn't hesitate to come to lunch at the Butterfly. I knew Goetz loved to eat and expected that I would fix something that he liked.

He picked at his mac with a fork. "I see you use breadcrumbs and something else."

"I put eggs in mine along with heavy cream instead of milk."

"That's why this is so velvety. Very good comfort food on this cold day. Great choice. Why did you come back so soon after . . . ?" He left unspoken the horrible murder/suicide of Doreen DeWitt and Lacey Bridges, which had taken place right in front of me in a church. It had been a terrible experience for everyone involved that day, and I had run to New York hoping to dispel those memories with new ones of living in the city that never sleeps. Goetz took a big bite of the casserole.

"I didn't want to spend the holidays alone in New York."

That explanation seemed to satisfy him. "I'm going to my daughter's home for Thanksgiving. My boy's family is joining us there." Goetz took another huge bite. "My daughter is a wonderful cook and she decorates the house real nice."

"Will your ex-wife be joining you?"

"I still don't want anything to do with her, so she alternates holidays with me. You know, one year I spend

Thanksgiving with the kids, then Christmas the next. Then we switch again. That way, we get to spend time with our kids and never have to deal with each other. The kids seem okay with it. Anything to avoid fighting. Getting back to Mrs. Bradley–I didn't say she was wrong. I just said that she didn't have enough for the police to go on."

"What do you think of the advice to hire a private investigator?"

"I think that's the way to go. Can she afford one?"

"Not an expensive one."

Goetz pulled out his notebook from his shirt pocket. With a stubby pencil, he wrote down a name along with a phone number. "Call this guy. Use my name. He owes me some favors. Tell him I'm calling one in."

I looked at the name. "Is he any good?"

"Very, but eccentric."

"Who isn't around here? Must be something in the water." I looked at the name and then at Goetz. "You've got to be kidding. This is his real name?"

"Yep. What's the problem?"

"It's just he has the same name as the character in *Double Indemnity*."

"Never read the book, but saw the film with Fred MacMurray and Barbara Stanwyck. Lots of people have the same names as famous characters in books and movies."

"Yeah? Ever run into anyone with this name before?"

"So—he's a mystery nut."

"Apparently his mother was."

"You're making too much of it."

"I just hope this detective's character is not like the guy in the book. A double crosser."

"He probably doesn't even know about his name. It's nothing. Just a coincidence." Goetz reached for the casserole dish and, finding it empty, looked disappointed. Taking his fork, Goetz scraped his plate free of any remaining cheese. Satisfied that he had eaten the last bit possible, he looked up smiling and asked, "What's for dessert?"

Thank goodness I had a chocolate mousse cake with caramel icing ready with ice-cold milk from the Farmers' Market.

Like I said—the man loved to eat.

4

Giles scratched on the door of the drawing room where Lady Elsmere, Mrs. Bradley and I waited.

"I hate that old French custom of scratching on doors," I complained. "It's like fingernails on a blackboard."

"Yes, Giles?"

"A Walter Neff to see you, Madam,"

"Please send him in. Oh, Giles, please knock next time. Mrs. Reynolds dislikes the continental way of doing things. She has a bad habit of blaming things she doesn't like on the French."

Giles nodded and went to fetch Mr. Neff, who was cooling his heels in the foyer.

"Now, Josiah, you do all the talking," coaxed Lady Elsmere.

"Yes, please," echoed Mrs. Bradley. "I don't know what to ask."

Our heads swiveled toward the massive walnut door as it opened. Giles and a squat, balding man, with what little hair he had left pulled back into a ponytail, strode into the room. I am also very sorry to inform you that he was wearing a white T-shirt under a pale green suit coat and expensive slip-on shoes with no socks. Apparently he had never gotten over *Miami Vice*. And to make matters worse, a gold chain hung from his neck.

"Oh," squeaked Mrs. Bradley in obvious disappointment.

I had to agree that Mr. Neff didn't look much like a detective. Where was the trench coat?

Mr. Neff, not noticing our dismay at his appearance, quipped, "You can tell my sidekick here that he can leave now. I'm not going to steal the family silver, at least not with you dames in the room anyway."

"Dames?" I repeated. That slang sent a shiver up my spine. I knew of another man from my past that had used '40s slang and might be indirectly responsible for my fall and another man's murder. You remember Larry Bingham.

"You may go now, Giles," said Lady Elsmere.

"Yeah, thanks for the jollies, Jeeves, Giles, James, whatever your name is," sneered Neff as he unwrapped a piece of chewing gum. After sticking gum between his wide puffy lips, he chewed as a cow chewing her cud while observing us. "Which one of you broads thinks she's being knocked off soon?"

"Mr. Neff, are you late for a belated Halloween party?" asked Lady Elsmere, gazing at him above her Versace glasses.

"Why would you ask that?"

"I should have thought it was rather obvious," stated Lady Elsmere, her expression hardening.

"She wants to know what in the hell . . . I mean, Lady Elsmere would like to ascertain if this is your regular mode of dress?" I asked, cutting in.

Neff gave a wide grin. "So you're the one I really talk to," he spouted, grinning at me. "Is there something wrong with my attire?" Neff held open his jacket and pranced around in a circle like a runway model.

"It's just that your outfit went out in the late '80s. How do you blend in when you are shadowing someone? Don't you stick out?"

"Ladies, this is my going-to-meetin'-clients outfit. I have reconnaissance attire. You don't need to worry about my professionalism. I'll get the job done." He pulled a chair over and sat down in front of us. "Gee, my feelings are hurt." He tugged at the shirt.

"And what's with the name?"

"What do you mean, Josiah?" asked Lady Elsmere, hostilely eying the scratch on the floor made by the dragged chair.

"Josiah? Is that your name, Toots? Josiah. Isn't that a boy's name?" he mocked. "Yeah, a king's name, isn't it? You think you're royalty or somethin'?"

"At least I'm not named after a movie character," I countered.

Neff clapped his hands in appreciation and gave a short whistle. "Someone knows her classic mystery movies." He winked at me.

"Her novels," quipped Lady Elsmere, under her breath.

"What's that?" asked Ethel confused.

"Nothing. Please continue," replied Lady Elsmere watching Josiah and Mr. Neff go after each other like two pigs fighting under a blanket.

"Walter Neff is the name of the murderous insurance man in the novel *Double Indemnity* by James M. Cain," I explained. "It was made into a movie with Barbara Stanwyck and Fred MacMurray in 1944, and is still considered today an almost perfect movie. It is numbered by the American Film Institute twenty-ninth out of the one hundred greatest films ever made and the book is considered a classic."

"How extraordinary!" exclaimed Lady Elsmere. "As if anyone would know that besides you, Josiah."

Neff gave a little shrug, smiling. "What can I say? My mom loved mystery stories. She named me after one of her favorite characters," he said to me.

Re-directing his attention, Neff looked directly at Ethel. "You must be the little lady who thinks someone is trying to "off" her."

Ethel nodded her blue-gray head, as she was too bewildered to speak.

"Let's get down to business. I told you my rates over the phone. If you give me your address, I shall start looking things over and report back in several days."

"We will only keep you on retainer for two days, Mr. Neff. That should be enough time to discover some information that would be useful," I interrupted.

Neff cracked his gum. "Is it? Well, I won't fight with the boss, which is obviously you," stated Neff. "I should have something for you in two days."

Lady Elsmere stood up. "Then you two can finish up the details. Ethel and I are not needed here."

Ethel echoed Lady Elsmere's cue. "No, not needed."

"I really should interview you, Ethel," suggested Neff. He grinned at her while smacking his gum.

"I've told Josiah everything."

Neff made a short rude sound with his mouth. "Okay, if that's the way you want to play this."

Lady Elsmere strode out of the room with Ethel trotting closely behind her, glancing nervously at Neff.

I thought he needed to interview Ethel too, but apparently Lady Elsmere had had enough of him. Sometimes she was like that with people . . . just cut them off. I made a suggestion. "Why don't you drop by this afternoon about tea time. I'll have her ready to talk to you then. She's a little nervous now. If you have a contract, please leave it on table."

"What was her name again?"

"Mrs. Bradley. Probably still is. You wanted to interview her, didn't you?"

"Yeah, I did, but I'm sort of getting over the idea, if you know what I mean." Neff leered at me.

Without thinking, I replied, "There's a speed limit in this state, Mr. Neff."

"How fast was I going, Officer?"

"I'd say around ninety."

"Suppose you get down off your motorcycle and give me a ticket?"

"Suppose I let you off with a warning this time."

"Suppose it doesn't take?"

"Suppose I have to whack you over the knuckles."

"Suppose I bust out crying and put my head on your shoulder."

"Suppose you try putting it on your client's shoulder."

"That tears it."

I put my fingers to my lips. "Oh my gosh. I can't believe we just did that."

Neff pushed his chair closer. "Yeah, I thought only nerds like me memorized dialogue from *Double Indemnity*, not beautiful dames like yourself. Must be awful lonely at nights, huh?" He leaned toward me and gave me the once-over. "Just think how good we'd be at other things."

My skin crawled. "Tea is served at four-thirty. I'll make sure that Mrs. Bradley has her wits about her and has written down the important facts."

"You gonna be here, Toots?"

"No, Mr. Neff. I have my own mystery movie to star in."

"Too bad. We could have made beautiful music together."

"I assure you that is just in *your* imagination."

"And, oh, what an imagination I have!" He gave me the once-over again. "I like women with a little meat on them."

"Mr. Neff, go to the door. Put your hand on the knob. Turn it to the left. Now please walk–not slither–out the door."

"See you around, Toots," said Mr. Neff as he moved into the hallway. He turned to say something else.

I slammed the door in his face.

5

"I'm not going to increase your dosage or switch medications."

"Then you don't believe me."

"It's not a matter of believing you, Mrs. Reynolds. It's just that I can't find anything wrong with you. I think you are experiencing what is called phantom pain. There is no physical reason that I can find for increasing your dosage."

"If I were a man, you'd increase it."

"That's ridiculous."

"I'm in pain. Now what are you going to do?"

"I am suggesting that you learn to live with it."

"Why don't I crack your leg with my cane and you learn to live with the pain?"

"Are you threatening me?"

"No, I'm begging you."

"I suggest that you try alternative methods like meditation, acupuncture or hypnosis."

"You've got to be kidding me!"

"Don't you understand that you are a borderline addict? If I increase your medication or switch to hardcore narcotics, then three months from now, I'll be sending you to Betty Ford, plus I'll lose my license."

"Other states have more humane attitudes toward those in pain."

"Other states don't have the drug problem we have. Other states actually pay their own way. They're not an entitlement state like we have become. We get more funding from the federal government than we send to Washington, which is why I will never understand the reason this state always votes red in national elections. But a lot of the need for this entitlement money is due to drug abuse, not because people can't find jobs."

"So now I am a drag on society."

"You're becoming a drag with me. You're not going to get a different prescription. That's final!" said the doctor on his way out the door.

That went well.

6

I was changing my bed sheets when Baby decided to help me . . . again. His idea of help was chasing his tail, getting between the bed and me, and trying to eat a pillowcase.

"That's it. Out you go," I declared. I had only so much energy to do housework and Baby wasted a lot of it . . . being Baby. I was trying to open the patio door and pull Baby outside by his collar at the same time. Big mistake.

The result was that the door cracked open enough to let Baby's kittens rush in with their mother following behind them. She immediately jumped in my Hans Wegner Papa Bear chair for a nap.

Once they could fend for themselves I had the kittens neutered and placed in the barn. The problem was they never stayed there.

Of course Baby was delighted that his comrades in mischief had breached the Butterfly. Barking loudly, he played with the kittens, which included chasing them up my leg and onto my head.

"Damn it," I cursed, trying to disengage a kitten's entrenched claws from my hair.

"Uhmmm," said Eunice, looking amused in the doorway.

"Can you get this cat off my head? His claws are digging into my scalp!" I cried out in frustration.

Eunice threw the cat on the floor and then turned her attention to Baby. "Baby, be quiet!"

The Mastiff immediately quit howling and sat on the floor looking up inquisitively at Eunice.

"Why does that dog obey everyone but me?" I questioned while straightening my hair in the dresser mirror.

"It's a phase. He's a teenager. No teenage boy listens to his mother," responded Eunice, glancing about at the mayhem the cats were creating by knocking items off nightstands and darting in and out from beneath the bed. She handed me a card.

"What's this?"

"A Sir Anthony is here to see you."

"Without an appointment? How dare he," I cracked.

"Be careful with this one. I don't think he'll understand your sense of humor."

"What does he want?"

"Didn't say. Just wants to see you." Eunice glanced at her hair in the mirror also. "You know, he seems awfully familiar. I wonder if he came to my hotel in Bermuda."

"Ask him."

"I can hardly do that, Josiah. There are some things that you just don't ask."

I shrugged. "Do I look okay enough to see one of England's noble gentry?"

"No, but you'll have to do. Now get out there and see what he wants."

Putting on some lipstick, I gave myself one last look in the mirror before going into the great room. There I found Sir Anthony studying my art collection. He turned at my approach. I took stock of him.

Sir Anthony was of the typical aristocratic Norman-Saxon appearance–broad forehead, Roman nose, tall, high color, blue eyes, slightly balding. One could see Viking and Germanic blood co-mingling with Celtic de sang pulsating through his slim frame. Of course, the haughtiness he exuded had been drilled into English schoolboys ever since Admiral Lord Nelson triumphed over the French and Spanish navies at the Battle of Trafalgar. To these chaps–God is an Englishman.

"Hello," I said pleasantly. "I'm Josiah Reynolds." I held out my hand.

Sir Anthony took it and kissed the air above my Clorox-scented hand. "I am Sir Anthony Preston Gladwyne, Lady Elsmere's nephew."

"Yes, I know. Would you like to sit down, Sir Anthony?"

"Thank you very much."

"Would you like tea or perhaps coffee?"

"No thank you. I know it's close to teatime, but I find that a really well brewed tea can be found only in Great Britain, although I tip my hat to you Yanks for your coffee. I'll have my man make me some tea when I get back to the cottage."

So Lady Elsmere's huge antebellum mansion was a "cottage."

I turned to Eunice, who was listening in the doorway. "We don't need anything. Thank you."

Eunice gave Sir Anthony a stony eye before leaving the room.

"I take it this is not a social visit."

"No shilly-shally here, eh?"

"We Americans like plain talk. What can I do for you?"

"I wanted to discuss a matter of delicacy about which you can be immensely helpful."

"Okay. Spill."

"Pardon?"

"Let's have it."

"Oh, yes. Straight to the point, eh?"

I sat in my chair taking Sir Anthony in. His shirt cuffs looked a little frayed.

"When I came to visit my great-aunt, I was horrified at the condition in which she lived."

"I don't understand what you mean?"

"The house was a mess and totally disorganized. My man, Giles, has tried his best to get the house in some sort of order, but has had his hands tied by this chap Charles and his family—the DuPuys.

"Since I am a family member, it is my duty to make sure that Lord Elsmere's widow be cared for in the manner fitting her station."

"Sir Anthony," I said, butting in. "I know that employees in America are not as deferential as in England and things move a little slower here, but I can assure you that Lady Elsmere's household runs at peak efficiency and her Ladyship is under the best of care."

"I beg to differ. The food was inedible when I came. I had to hire new cooks. Expensive wine has disappeared from the wine cellar as well as personal items such as my pocket watch, which had been in my family since the eighteenth century. Even her Ladyship's unmentionables were not washed and mended. She has had to do without. It's disgraceful."

The thought of June going without bloomers made me smile.

"This is no laughing matter."

"I can see that. There may be a period of adjustment if Charles has to devote all his time to the farm now and not to the house, but things will even out. Charles will make sure of it."

"I'm afraid I can't take your word for it. Something must be done."

Here was the crux of the conversation. I already knew what he was going to suggest before he spewed it out into the room.

"I am of the opinion that this DuPuy family is taking advantage of my good aunt and something should be done."

"Like what?"

"I think they should be removed from positions of authority as they are not competent."

"Why are you telling me this?"

"Because I know that you are very close to this family and were instrumental in having Lady Elsmere declare Charles her immediate heir."

"The DuPuy family is aristocracy around here. They worked for Henry Clay's family and helped build this community, even in the dark years."

"They are descendants of slaves and have no relationship to my aunt other than being servants."

Pursing my lips, I asked evenly, "Why tell me?"

"Because changes have to be made and they should be discreet."

"In other words—you're telling me to butt out."

Sir Anthony's face took on a flinty quality. "This is a private family matter. Outside interference will be resisted."

I stood up. "Thank you, Sir Anthony. I understand precisely where you're coming from."

He stood also. "I trust that we have an understanding as we both have Lady Elsmere's best interests at heart."

"I do have Lady Elsmere's best interests at heart."

"Good. Your cooperation will be greatly appreciated. It's really for the greater good."

"May I see you out?"

Taking the hint, Sir Anthony held up his hand. "Thank you for taking the time to talk with me. I can see that I disrupted cleaning day."

I returned a weak smile. I think he had just taken a stab at me.

It was at this time that Eunice let Baby out of the bedroom. He padded happily into the great room to see who was visiting. In his mouth, he held one of the kittens.

Sir Anthony's blue eyes widened. "Goodness! What is that Mastiff going to do with that feline?"

"Eat it. It's dinner."

Eunice held the front door open as Sir Anthony gave one last ghastly look at Baby before hurrying out.

Disappointed that he couldn't show off his trophy, Baby spat out the cat and began giving her a bath with his huge tongue. Purring, the cat settled under Baby's expert nurturing.

Laughing, I patted Baby on his massive head.

"Can you believe that man's gall?" blurted Eunice.

"Something not kosher is going on. I assumed you listened to the entire conversation."

"Absolutely. I know that I've seen that man before."

"I'm going to have a long talk with Charles. He needs to be warned," I said.

"I'm going to look through all my papers from my time in Bermuda. I know it was there that I've seen him."

"Good. Let me know if you find something."

"Did you hear the contempt in his voice when he was talking about Charles' family?" Eunice asked.

"Don't take it personally. It's not about race. It's about class. Sir Anthony probably scores high on the narcissism chart and thinks everyone else is on the planet to cater to those of his station. I know he and his man are lying about something. For one thing, his man said his name was Giles. Now Giles' accent sounds Irish to me and no good Irishman would take on an English name without cause. I think the name is phony. We need to get a look at that guy's passport."

Eunice kidded, "I'm sure you will arrange that somehow. Thank goodness you are on the side of the angels, Josiah. I'd hate to see you slide over to the devil's side.

I turned to Eunice. "Don't think that because I'm on the side of angels, I actually am one."

I wasn't kidding.

I was serious.

Dead serious.

7

Shaneika Mary Todd stood at her office window, scrutinizing Cheapside Park below, which was located to the left of the old courthouse facing Main Street.

She wondered how many people knew that the park with its tired fountain and patchy grass held a statue of an ancestor of hers–slave owner John C. Breckinridge.

John C. was a devoted believer in slavery and opposed any dismantling of legal protection for it. He served as Vice President of the United States, ran for President in 1860, and became Secretary of War for the Confederacy during the Civil War. Yet he represented freed slaves in court, protecting their rights while supporting voluntary emancipation.

When he visited his cousin, Mary Todd, in Lexington he met Abraham Lincoln and they became good friends despite their political differences until the Civil War came.

So that a statue of such a complex man should stand on the site of the busiest slave market in the nation prior to 1860, second only to New Orleans, was fitting. Slavery was a complex issue.

Kentucky had the third-largest number of slave owners in the Union with 38,385 households owning an average of five or more slaves. Even the state's song, *My Old Kentucky Home*, is connected to slavery. Stephen Foster first called it *Poor Uncle Tom, Good Night;* a possible expression of sold slaves mourning for their Kentucky home.

In the middle of the park had stood a wooden block where slaves were auctioned, while over in another corner had been a whipping post for those who resisted being bought.

Some of Shaneika's ancestors certainly were sold there. And some of her ancestors bought there. There were dark stories on both sides.

Besides her passion for Thoroughbred racing Shaneika loved history, especially that of her esteemed family and the locale. Sometimes she gave talks to schools about the history of slavery and indentured servitude in Kentucky and compared it to human trafficking today.

She tried to give both slave owners and slaves a human face. Shaneika knew from bills of sale stored in her office safe that as soon as some of her relatives got their freedom, they ventured to Cheapside to buy a slave of their own before the Union boys shut the market down. Sometimes a free black person would buy a white person who had sold himself into slavery, as he was no longer able to fend for himself. The most famous case of this was Aunt Charlotte and William King Solomon in the 1830s.

How complex human nature is, Shaneika thought. Would she, a freed slave in the early nineteenth century, have bought another human being at Cheapside if given the opportunity?

Her great, great, great aunt had done so, and the slave had died under her neglectful care. It was one of those dirty little stories in the family.

Post Civil War, former slaves' lives were in some ways worse, as they did not have their masters' legal protection.

Many whites could not accept the emancipation decree. The Ku Klux Clan raged against the former slave class in rural areas by sticking victims' heads on pikes along the roadside as a warning to other blacks.

Newly emancipated slaves fled to Lexington seeking protection in newly formed black neighborhoods while others went further north to escape the violence.

Life was harsh for people of color in the Lexington area especially.

Between 1882 and 1968 there were over two hundred lynchings in Kentucky. Records show that one hundred people were lynched within a fifty-mile radius of Lexington.

While the majority of the victims were African American males, white men and black women were also lynched.

Many white men were hung because they were trying to stop a lynching, but African American women were lynched just for being "uppity." It didn't matter if they were in the right.

In 1904, Marie Thompson of Shepherdsville, Kentucky was attacked by John Irvin, her landlord, with a knife. Being a woman of substance, Marie got the knife during the struggle and slit Irvin's throat. She was arrested for murder, but Marie never got to trial.

She was busted out of jail by a lynch mob who hung her. As she swung in the air, Marie grabbed one of her attackers by the collar and grabbed his knife. Then she reached up and cut the hemp rope. Fighting through a crowd of drunken men, she was finally gunned down. One hundred shots were fired at her. Marie Thompson suffered and then died the next day in jail from gunshot wounds.

Even those who were convicted and sentenced to die by the electric chair still had to fear the lynch mob.

In 1920 a little white girl, Geneva Hardman, was beaten to death with a rock on her way to school.

Will Lockett, an African-American man, confessed to the murder. He was also responsible for the murders of three other women.

But even though he was convicted, a lynch mob formed. The National Guard was called in and the riot that ensued left five people dead and fifty wounded. Martial law was declared in Lexington.

This was the first time Southern authorities took a public stand. Lexington was the first city in the South to try to officially stop lynching and Kentucky was the first state to make anti-lynching the law of the land.

Shaneika shuddered. How much blood had that park soaked up the past two hundred years? And the Native Americans fighting here even before the European and African era added to the town's bloodletting history.

She had heard rumors recently that the city had plans to build a pavilion there for entertainment purposes and to house the Farmers' Market on Saturdays. Her cheeks twitched as she thought of young kids strumming guitars and people selling tomatoes where lives had been destroyed.

But perhaps everyone should forget the past in Lexington and just get on with the business of living.

That's the advice she was going to give Josiah Reynolds. "Be glad that you are alive and keep going forward." That is . . . after she gave her the bad news. Fred O'nan was free!

In a plea bargain, Fred O'nan had entered an Alford plea of guilty. The Alford plea is a catch-22. You can plead guilty and yet not be guilty. It was just a way for a defendant to say that he had had enough fighting the courts, and the court's way of saying they didn't have enough evidence to convict or didn't really believe the defendant was guilty. Either way, the books could be closed on the case and everyone was happy.

The judge still had the power either to give O'nan a sentence or set him free, but everyone knew this judge had never liked the case. It had to do with the lack of "mirandizing" O'nan until he had set foot on American soil. The judge felt O'nan had a good case of kidnapping on foreign territory if he had chosen to pursue it, but with the Alford plea–that possibility ended. Basically, the judge slapped O'nan's hand with a ruler.

But still there were some parameters that O'nan had to observe.

He couldn't come within a hundred feet of Josiah or her property.

The same with Franklin.

He couldn't sue the city, Josiah Reynolds, Franklin or the police department for his dismissal in either criminal or civil court.

He had to attend psychiatric sessions for six months and then the court would review his progress. The court felt O'nan had anger problems with middle-aged women.

He was on probation for three years.

But Fred O'nan would not serve one more day in jail. His tracking bracelet would be removed, and as long as he observed the terms of his release, he was basically a free man.

The DA had wanted to call Josiah and inform her, but Shaneika stopped her. Over the past year, Shaneika had come to know Josiah Reynolds and what made her tick.

Shaneika knew that Josiah skirted around the law when it suited her, but down deep Josiah would do what she thought was the righteous thing to do.

In Kentucky that could be different from book law. There was the law and then there was Kentucky justice.

Shaneika knew that Josiah was going to take this hard.

Very hard!

8

I didn't know how to respond. I just stared at Shaneika with a silly expression on my face that somehow corresponded to "duh?"

We sat in silence until Eunice Todd unclasped her hands only to flutter one hand about her neck. The gesture made me flinch. "I think I will make some tea." She rose and went into the kitchen.

"Does Franklin know?" I asked.

"Yes, I spoke to him earlier. He's coming out here later on. He wants to talk to you about it. I told him it would be all right. That is okay, isn't it?"

"Of course. Franklin is always welcome."

"I told you that this judge was quirky and very pro-police. He thinks O'nan's rights were violated."

"That man tried to kill Franklin and me and then ran off to a foreign country. What about our rights!"

"I know. I know. You don't have to tell me this stinks."

"I know you warned me, but I didn't think in my wildest dreams that this judge would really let O'nan go. No prison time. None! Surely there is something that can be done about this?"

"No, there isn't. And you stay away from both the judge and O'nan."

"What about a civil suit? O'nan had to be getting money from somewhere to hide that long."

"I wouldn't advise it. It's over. I know it's not fair, but I've seen burglars that have broken into people's houses sue the victims if they got hurt during the process, like falling over toys and breaking a leg. And the burglars won their cases. You can never tell what is going to happen with a judge or a jury. Let it go, I'm tellin' you. Let it go."

"What if he comes back to finish the job?"

Shaneika shook her head in exasperation.

Eunice put down a tray and handed a cup to Josiah. "She won't say it, but I will. Then you'll have to kill him and make it look right for the law."

"Mother!"

"Don't *mother* me. The woman has a right to be concerned. The law does very little to protect women in this state. Husbands and boyfriends kill their women folk all the time. You know as well as I do that they sometimes get off even with lots of evidence against them."

Eunice reached over and patted my knee. "I know that the thought is repulsive to a decent person, but if the time comes and your life or someone you love is in danger, instinct will kick in. You will do what needs to be done."

"You said you thought he was high that night, Josiah?" asked Shaneika.

"Yes, his eyes were dilated and his skin looked flushed."

"He has to do talk therapy as part of his probation. Maybe he's calmed down and will work this out. Maybe he will forget about you."

"Fred O'nan taking responsibility for his own screw-ups is about as probable as a dog in a manger."

Shaneika smiled. "Mom always uses that phrase, but I have never understood what it means."

"Sweetie, it means that the dog can't eat the hay in the manger, but doesn't allow other animals to eat it either, just out of pure meanness," explained Eunice.

"Eunice, you were right about living my life," I announced. "We are going to proceed with the weddings and open the Butterfly. The truth is if someone wants to get you, locked doors and security cameras aren't going to keep them out. They will find a way in sooner or later. I know that from my daughter's work.

"I'm only fifty-one. I just can't curl up and die, waiting for the boogie man."

"You're way too young for that," concurred Eunice.

I took a sip of tea. "You know this would taste better with some of my honey."

"I knew there was something I forgot," stated Eunice, looking happier.

Wanting to change the subject, I glanced at Shaneika and admired her new haircut. It was cut very close to the scalp. "Every time I see you, you have a new hairdo."

"You like it?"

"Yes, I'm very glad you cut off those dreadlocks."

"Too ethnic for a white girl like you to appreciate?"

"They looked uncomfortable."

Shaneika laughed. "Don't tell anyone but when my scalp itched, I couldn't scratch it. It was driving me crazy." She laughed again.

The image of silver bells falling over waterfalls filled my mind as to describe her laughter. Shaneika rarely laughed. She should laugh more as it was lovely.

"I'm so glad that you're taking this much better than I thought you would. It would be in everyone's best interests if you could calm Franklin down when he comes. He was very agitated when I left him."

Nodding, I assured Shaneika, "I will take care of Franklin. You leave him to me." I took another sip of my tea. As far as I was concerned the conversation was over . . . at least where Shaneika was concerned.

When Eunice and Shaneika left, I called my daughter's secret private number. Someone picked it up but said nothing. I could hear breathing on the other end of the phone.

"Rosebud," was all I said.

9

"Franklin, get the hell out of my closet!" I yelled.

"I spent all that time getting clothes for you that fit and look stylish, and you turn around wearing granny clothes again. I will not be seen in public with you looking like that."

"I have to wear clothes that are easy to get on and off. I can't wear things that have zippers or too many buttons. Sometimes those types of clothes are not the most trendy, but they are comfortable and easy for me."

Franklin gave me a blank stare. "Blah, blah, blah. You'll never catch a man looking like that."

"What would I want with a man at this stage of my life?"

"It's only been a month or so since Jake left and now you are taking vows of chastity? Oh come on, honey gal.

You two were probably doing the nasty all the time. I
know you better than that. That one leg might not be
working so hot, but what's between those legs is doing
just fine."

I turned away. There was no way I was going to
wrangle Franklin out of my closet and I didn't want to
discuss Jake. The thought of him leaving still hurt deeply.
How could I have been so stupid as to fall in love at my
age!

"Oh, goodness!"

"What!"

"Are you wearing these huge granny panties again, and
here is one with a hole." Franklin held out the offending
garment. "Trash bag, sister."

"How come you are so duded up?" I asked, wanting to
change the subject again.

Franklin was wearing black pants, a dove gray shirt
with a silver tie, black hard-sole shoes, and belt. He
looked smart, successful, and grown-up. Very
conservative. Not at all like his usual getups. "I had a job
interview in Cincinnati."

"Really?"

"Yes, really," he replied, throwing a beloved pair of my
stretch pants over his shoulder. "And I have another
interview in New York next week."

"Running away, huh?"

Franklin gave me a contemptuous look. "I knew you'd
say that. I'm not running away. I'm running to

something. There's nothing for me here, and yes, if the truth were known, I'd rather not be in the same town with that lunatic O'nan having free reign. Sometimes it's best to move on. That's what I'm doing."

He looked at some old pantyhose and ripped them apart. "No one wears these anymore. And you should do the same."

"Same what?"

"Move on."

Franklin moved over to my jewelry box.

"Can't. Dug in."

"Go live in London with Asa."

"What about all my animals?"

Franklin started trying on my necklaces and rings. "This is costume jewelry. Where's all the good stuff?"

"Around the neck of Brannon's mistress."

"OOOOH. Sorry. Didn't think before I spoke." He admired himself in the closet mirror. "Have Charles' grandsons live here while you're gone."

"Are you nuts? The whole place would be trashed. They're barely twenty. There would be a party here every night."

"I'm just telling you that a plan is needed. None of this thinking everything is gonna be all right if you just sit on your fanny. You need to be proactive."

"Franklin, take that brooch out of your pocket and put it back in my jewelry box."

"You never wear it. It's just going to waste. I have a

'70s yellow jumpsuit that it would look sweet on."

There was a knock on the closet door. Both our heads swiveled. Standing in the doorway lounged Matt, wearing a gray flannel suit with a crisp white shirt accented by a charcoal tie with red stripes. His hair was freshly combed and nails manicured, with expensive cologne subtly drifting toward us. He looked like a model out of a magazine.

I stopped breathing for a moment.

"Mind if I come in?" he asked. He directed his gaze toward Franklin.

Franklin swirled furiously in my direction. "Did you plan this?"

"Heavens no. I've got enough on my plate without setting up a cat fight between the two of you, but since he's here, you can beat the crap out of him." I pushed Franklin toward Matt. "Go for it!"

I do not believe in zero tolerance toward violence.

Sometimes two people just had to duke it out. Besides, I thought Matt had it coming. There stood Franklin trembling with his hands balled into fists facing a much taller and heavier Matt leaning against the door jamb. However, a scrawny cat can whip a much bigger dog if it's determined.

"Didn't come here to fight you or Franklin. I heard what the judge did and came to offer help, but if neither of you wants it," he said as he began walking away.

"Why did you do it, Matt?" blurted out Franklin.

Matt whipped around, facing Franklin. "I never said

our arrangement was permanent. I wanted to stay friends, but you declined. *You* broke up our friendship."

"You said you loved me. Were you lying?"

"I did love you and still do, but I want what most men want. A family. I don't want to do the bar scene anymore or be around neurotic screaming fags."

Franklin gasped. "Is that what you think I am? Just one of those effeminate gay men who are divas. You're the diva, Matt.

"I accepted everything you threw at me. You were never faithful. A cat in heat is more discriminating than you are and it didn't make any difference if they were men or women, as long as they could help you get something. But I never said a word, even when you hooked up with Josiah."

Matt's eyes widened almost imperceptibly, but he said nothing.

I should have defended Matt then, but I didn't. Our being together was my fault—not his. I was afraid if I said something on behalf of Matt that Franklin would turn on me. I can be such a little shit.

"Oh, you thought I didn't know about that little indiscretion. You're nothing but a hound. Please don't bother to deny it," accused Franklin.

"We never had an agreement about being exclusive."

"But that didn't keep you from using me. Since I've met you, I've been shot. Then, as soon as I could hold a rake, you had me working on this forsaken farm."

"You could have said no. You're blaming me for decisions you made," defended Matt.

"Cut the lawyer crap, please. You knew I would just to please you. I did everything you asked. You said–go to Key West and take Baby, so I dropped everything and went to Key West. You wouldn't move into town, so I helped you remodel that shack you live in. But all the fine details, the workmanship in that little hovel are due to me because you have no imagination. When it comes to clothes, colors, picking out a hot car, remodeling a house, books, landscaping–you are as dull as dishwater. You just buy whatever other people have or the most expensive, because you have no taste of your own–no imagination.

"And conversation? You know a little about art and wine. That's it. If a book hasn't been on Oprah's list, you are totally clueless.

"Dull, dull, dull. You're not the all-to-be-all, Matt. You're good-looking; that's it."

"Then why are you so mad, Franklin? You don't return my calls or emails. I have tried many times to contact you, but you refused to answer. Yet you stand accusing me of being a creep. Why all the energy if I'm so stupid?"

"Because you can't control with whom you fall in love. Believe me, I would have chosen someone more dynamic, someone with more ooomph. The truth is that you're boring, sweetie."

Matt's face fell flat. The thought that someone deemed him to be less than perfect was a surprise. He was so used to people catering to him. A big surprise.

Franklin flopped dramatically on the bed. "I really wish I could love someone else. I really do. I knew when

I met you that you would not be the joy of my life, but the undoing."

"Christ Almighty," muttered Matt, stunned. "I never knew you felt that way. Am I really boring?" Matt glanced at me.

I just shrugged.

"Believe me, I have prayed and prayed that God would take away these feelings for you, but it hasn't happened. I'm stuck," complained Franklin.

"Franklin, I had no idea. I don't know what to say. I told you from the get-go that I wanted a family of my own and that I was struggling. I took it for granted that someday I would move on, but always thought we'd still be friends. I didn't realize that you were so invested in our relationship."

"You broke my heart, Matt. You simply undid me."

Matt struggled for words. His eyes looked moist and conveyed a worried look as though he had suddenly realized something important.

"Tell me something, Matt. If you had married, would you have been faithful?"

"Yes. I would have tried to be so."

"There's that word–tried. You know men with homosexual tendencies can't be faithful to their wives. They'll always come back to their own kind."

"That's rubbish, Franklin. I don't know that and neither do you."

"Matt, we don't get to pick who we are, whom we love or who loves us. We can only cope as best we can with what we're given.

"It's different for each of us. For Josiah, it's her leg pain and the loss of her husband. For me, it's you. Those are our crosses to bear and we bear them as best we can. Not always perfect, but still forward."

"You've always been a proud gay man," countered Matt. "But who are you to tell me that I won't be able to live a life with a wife and kids? People are not tied to fate or labels. We each make our own decisions on how we want to live our lives."

"Man, are you drunk? What planet do you live on? You are what you are," accused Franklin. "You need to make peace with it." Sighing, he rose from the bed. "Whatever happened to Miss Mystery Writer anyway?"

"You know damned well Meriah hightailed it back to California without so much a fare-thee-well," snarled Matt.

Franklin smirked, "Awww, that's too bad. Isn't that awful, Josiah?"

I wiped my tearing eyes with a pair of ripped panties. All I could say was, "You guys!" and gave Franklin a big hug and then Matt, leaving them alone.

I had to admit it.

Franklin had just won the first round.

It was just what the doctor ordered for Matt.

10

Matt and Franklin were rummaging through my freezer looking for dinner. They had talked quietly for over an hour and now were famished.

I didn't know if they had made up or what the outcome was with them when the doorbell rang.

"Make sure you check the security monitor before you let someone in," I yelled from my office.

I heard murmurs and then the front door closed. Matt poked his head in my office. "There is a Walter Neff to see you. Has he seen *Double Indemnity* with Barbara Stanwyck?"

"Don't know," I replied. "I'll come out."

Entering the great room, I found Neff admiring my art collection. "Do you like art, Mr. Neff?"

"The closest I've ever come is putting a poster of *Starry Night* over my toilet."

"How charming."

"It covered a hole in the wall."

"Utilitarian, I see."

"Grab your coat, Toots."

"Why?"

"I've done a background check on the housekeeper and the nephew. It's the relative that turns up stinky. I want to go where he bought that lotto ticket and smooze around."

"Why do you need me?"

"The cashier is a woman. She'll be more likely to gossip with a another skirt rather than someone like me."

"You mean someone sleazy like you?"

"Toots, you cut me to the quick."

"I wonder if you even give a damn."

"I wonder if you wonder."

I scrunched up my nose. Neff had just said another famous quote from the movie dialogue of *Double Indemnity*. This was getting ridiculous. "Okay, but I can't do a long outing. I've got about two hours in me."

"That's enough time."

Matt came up behind me and helped put on my coat and handed me my cane and cell phone. "Yes, I was eavesdropping. Call me before you head home. Don't make me worry, please."

"Make sure you lock the house up tight when you leave," I requested.

"Stop by my house on the way home and I'll come back with you. I don't like you coming into an empty house by yourself."

"Jeez, what are you? Her father?" Neff turned toward Matt. "I'll get her back in one piece, Buster."

"See that you do, Shamus." (Shamus is a nickname for a private detective.)

"Everybody thinks he's a wise guy. Come on, Toots. Let's blow this popsicle stand." Intent on having the last word, Neff strode down the hallway and, throwing open the front door, made for his car which was a 1963 fire engine red Avanti with white detailing and lots and lots of mid-century polished chrome.

I caught my breath. I love beautiful things and this Avanti was made when America knew how to make great cars.

She had a white leather interior with red piping, red carpet and a red dashboard. To make a final statement, she had whitewall tires. She was so clean it looked like she had just come off the assembly line.

Avantis were the first cars to offer disc brakes and a fiberglass body. This was the same type of fiberglass that had been used for panels on the Chevrolet Corvette in 1953.

Fewer than five thousand Avantis were made in 1963. The problem was that the factory couldn't keep up with demand and the Avantis had to be discontinued.

He opened the car door for me before heading to the driver's side of the car. It was an unexpected gesture. Maybe Neff wasn't such a jerk after all.

"Franklin, come look at this," yelled Matt. "This knucklehead's got an Avanti."

"You lie!" cried Franklin from inside the house. I heard a chair scoot back.

Before we would be caught up in male adulation of American cars, I hurried into the Avanti. "Make tracks, daddeo," I commanded.

Neff grinned while leaving an opened-mouthed Franklin and Matt standing in the dust of my gravel driveway.

Laughter bubbled up from my throat until Neff swerved around one of my peacocks. "Man, if you hit one of my animals, I'm gonna knock you upside the head," I warned.

"Dig it," was all Neff replied as he sped out onto Route 169 heading toward Nicholasville. We then turned left onto Route 68, heading toward the Kentucky River.

"Where are we going?" I asked, enjoying the ride. Neff seemed to be a competent driver once out of my driveway.

"It turns out that Jubal Bradley is Ethel Bradley's only living relative. He's her husband's brother's boy. Both parents have been dead over ten years and Ethel has, from time to time, loaned him money."

"I see." I didn't remind him that I already knew this.

"He works in Versailles at the Sylvania plant and his boss told me that he is a good worker. Rarely takes a sick day off, but there are rumors that Jubal is in hot water. His boss's secretary told me that Jubal loves to play the ponies, and ran into trouble, having to borrow from a loan shark."

"When Ethel dies, everything goes to Jubal?"

"Bull's-eye. That's enough for motive. She may not have a lot, but there is a paid-for house, some savings, and a car. Maybe enough to satisfy Jubal's loan shark."

"If that story has legs to it."

"Exactly," Neff agreed.

"So why do you need me again?"

"It was that story about her house being searched. Now why was Jubal searching her house?"

"Looking for cash?"

"Ethel's strictly a bank gal. She writes checks and uses debit cards. At the most, she has a hundred in her purse for emergencies."

"Maybe a druggie got into her house."

"Then he would have turned it upside down looking for cash or drugs. Whoever went into her house didn't want her to know it was searched. He didn't buy on the old lady being so astute." Neff searched around his catchall and pulled out a pair of vintage aviator Ray-Bans. "Clean these off for me, will ya?"

I wiped them off with my skirt and handed them back.

"It was that her Bible had been moved. That's what piqued my interest. Why look in her Bible?"

"Because that's where she kept her lotto tickets," I replied.

Neff snapped his fingers. "Bingo. I'm thinking the lotto ticket wasn't in her Bible and he had to search the rest of the house."

"But then . . . why cut the brake line to her car?"

"I bet the intention was not to kill Ethel since she doesn't drive over forty miles an hour. Two possible explanations. Number one–to scare her into revealing the location of the lotto ticket or number two–the loan shark did it as a warning to Jubal."

"But Ethel said she didn't win. So what's the point?"

"I found out at the tea interview that you set up with Ethel that she didn't examine the ticket. She assumed the numbers were the ones she had dictated to Jubal. What if he bought two tickets and switched them accidentally, with his ticket winning the lotto?"

"Or that he put down the wrong numbers to begin with, but still won."

"Yeah. That's what you're going to find out. We're going to the store where Ethel gets her lotto tickets." Neff handed me a piece of paper. "These are the numbers she plays every week. You're going into the store and say that you are getting a ticket for Miss Ethel. Just talk it up and see what you can find out."

"Are you sure?"

"Come on. Women talk to women. The clerk might be guarded with me–a stranger and all."

"How do you know it's a woman?"

Neff rolled his eyes. "Because I asked Ethel. Now are you going to help me or not?"

"If you say please," I cooed.

"Good. Just do what I say. I can't stand all these questions. Yak. Yak. Yak."

"Ummm, you didn't say please."

"Really?"

"I must insist."

"Please will you help me? Pretty please with sugar on top."

"I would be delighted, Mr. Neff. There's no need to be sarcastic."

"I don't remember shamuses using please when telling their dolls what to do. They did it or got their noses mussed."

"My nose is fine as it is, thank you, and you are not in a Raymond Chandler lead role."

"You'd look swanky with your hair in a French twist wearing a black hat with a veil. You know, those hats from the '40s. Nothing sexier than watching a dame fold up her veil to put on some lipstick. Gives her an air of mystery."

"Oh really. I'll bite. What kind of dress?"

"A black dress accentuated with Joan Crawford shoulder pads and a low v-neckline, cinched in at the waist with a sparkling belt. A great dress for accenting a woman's breasts and hips. Then Dragon-red lipstick. Open-toed shoes with toes painted the same color."

"Shall I smoke as well?"

"Can't stand kissing dames with smoke on their breath. They should taste sweet like strawberries."

"I see. Would you like me to tell you what I like in a man?" I asked.

Neff gave me a cheeky grin before turning his attention back to the road. We were now on a very curvy stretch along the palisades, which needed his concentration.

"Cut the hair off. I mean all of it. Especially that ridiculous ponytail."

Neff started to protest.

"Shut up. You have had your turn. Again, cut the entire head. Your hair is not worth saving and bald men can be sexy. Shave. I mean every day and put on cologne. Wear clothes from this decade. Get rid of the jewelry except for a ring, and wax that obnoxious hair from your back and neck. It peeks out from your clothes. It's a wonder that you don't walk on all fours."

"Hey!"

"Women do not like hairy men. It reminds us too much of the cave era when we were chattel."

"You're not now? When did that change?"

"Cut your nails. Use mouthwash and lots of it. Wear clean underwear–every day. Do this and you might have a fighting chance with a female homo sapien. Not an overly bright female, but someone lower on the pay grade who is easily fooled."

Neff shook his head. "Naw. I'm too much as it is."

"I don't know how I keep my hands from wandering."

"I told you not to stifle yourself. Let go, baby. Explore the Neffman."

"The Neffman?"

"All yours for the taking, Toots."

"However shall I stand it?"

"You want me. You know you do." He put his hand on my knee. "Let's say we do the nasty after we visit that old biddy at the store. I'll get a hotel room. Even pay for it."

"What a gentleman!"

His hand started inching up my thigh. "What are you looking for?"

"My Taser and pepper spray," I replied, rummaging through my purse. "Ah, there it is." I pulled out my Taser and kissed it.

Neff pulled his hand away. "Very funny."

"You're all talk, anyway."

"Wanna bet?"

"Let me put it this way. If you were the last man on earth, this time I wouldn't have to be pushed off a cliff. I would jump of my own accord. Now you're wearing me out with your constant drivel. Shall we concentrate on the case?"

Walter Neff pursed his lips and popped some gum into his mouth.

After that, I refused to talk to him, although he mumbled frequently. I would catch a few words here and there like "think she is" and "stuck-up female." You know that bunch of cliché crap men spout when they don't get their way.

As I cracked open my window to let in some fresh air, I wondered if Neff was really serious or just yanking my chain. I wondered if he knew.

I wondered if he wondered.

11

We coasted into Harrodsburg, a small southern town of eight thousand souls. It was the first city founded in Kentucky and its fort was built even earlier than Fort Boonesborough, its more famous counterpart, by one year–1774. But nobody remembers its founder, James Harrod, while everyone knows of Daniel Boone, the founder of Boonesborough. Daniel Boone just had a better PR posse.

Harrodsburg's main claim today is an exact replica of the same fort built on some thirty-two acres right in the heart of the town. The only thing missing is the stench from the rude hygiene customs of the day. Pioneers used to say that one smelled a fort long before it came into view.

Of course, the replica fort also lacks the courtyard comprised entirely of mud, flies, and the filthy inhabitants that made up the fort. Today the fort's imprint encompasses a beautiful lawn, gift shop, sparkling clean cabins, and well-groomed re-enactors.

Another Harrodsburg highlight is the Beaumont Inn, a B&B that specializes in southern cooking. Walking into the main building is like walking into the past, as much of its nineteenth century furniture is still very much in use.

Beaumont Inn was built in 1845 as a college for well-bred young ladies–mainly those south of the Mason-Dixon line. Many upstanding families sent their daughters to this college during the Civil War to keep them out of harm's way while their parents fought for the "noble cause."

It was ironic that Kentucky's bloodiest battle during the Civil War was fought not fifteen miles from the school at a little hamlet called Perryville, where Ethel resided. Cannon fire was so fierce that windows in the town rattled.

Harrodsburg was used as a hospital center for many of the wounded of both sides as was Shakertown, a religious community devoted to work, prayer, and celibacy located north of Harrodsburg. The Shakers invented the clothespin, among other household items. That meant we girls were one step closer to the invention of the washing machine. Of course, anything would be better than beating clothes with rocks and clay at the river.

Neff pulled over while I mused over the directions written by Ethel and then pored over a map. "Turn left at the next corner," I directed, "and then go about four miles."

Pulling out into the traffic, Neff turned the car left and sped down a country lane. Finally seeing the little store that was our goal, he turned into the parking lot.

I got out of the Avanti and ventured into the store.

Wandering around the aisles, I finally decided upon a Moon Pie, which I hadn't had in years, and a Diet Rite Cola. Seeing that a sixtyish woman was overseeing the cash register, I made my move.

"Anything else, dearie?" the clerk asked, revealing very perfect teeth. Must be expensive caps, which might explain the overly tight clothes for a woman of her age. And yes, there was cleavage showing. This lady was fighting age and doing a nice job of it. She was holding her own.

"Yes, there is. I'm a friend of Ethel Bradley's and she asked me to get a lottery ticket for her. Let me see now. Ah yes, here are the numbers she wants me to play." I handed the lady a handwritten note from Ethel.

She raised her glasses and peered closely at it. "You kin to her?"

I raised my hand in deference. "No. She is staying in town with a friend, but she made me promise to come get this lottery ticket. Seems like it is very important to her."

The clerk leaned across the counter. "Oh, it is like lighting a candle for the dead, you see. She does it in memory of her husband and son. Both gone now for years."

"Oh, I didn't know."

"So you see why it is important to her."

"Yes. I'm so glad I came then. Your name is?"

"Suzy. I've been waiting on Miss Ethel going on twenty years now. She always plays the same numbers." Suzy glanced down at the note. "And these are the correct numbers," she confirmed. "I tried to tell Jubal that his numbers were wrong but he wouldn't listen."

"Jubal is . . . ?"

Suzy leaned on her elbows and glanced around the store. In a stage whisper, she confided, "That's Ethel's nephew. He came in last week or so to buy a ticket for Ethel, but gave the wrong numbers. I told him so. I have the numbers memorized by heart after all these years, but would he listen?" She shook her head. "He's a hard-headed man. Told me to mind my own business and kept insisting he wrote them down right, but he probably didn't listen to Ethel either."

"What happened?"

"I did my job."

"You sold him a ticket with the wrong numbers?"

"Wrong for Ethel, but maybe right for him." She winked at me.

"I'm sorry, but I don't know what that means."

"I checked the paper on Sunday and I couldn't remember all his numbers, but the numbers in the paper were close, so maybe he won something."

"Would that still be Ethel's win if she had paid for the ticket even if he gave the wrong numbers?"

"Yes, but he could go to court over it. I'm sure a judge would be sympathetic to both parties."

A customer came in and Suzy pulled up from the counter. The confidential gabfest was over.

"Do you still have Sunday's paper?" I asked.

"No dearie, we don't keep unsold papers."

"Thank you very much." I started out the door.

"Don't you want Ethel's ticket for this week?"

"How stupid of me. Yes. How much?"

We finished our transaction, and then I hurried to the Avanti where I gave Walter a brief rundown.

"We need a library or a computer," he spat out.

"We'll have to go to Danville now. It's closer."

"Didn't we just come through Harrodsburg?"

"Yes, but now Danville is closer. We've driven into the country several miles since Harrodsburg."

"Which way?"

"Turn onto Route 150. Danville is a college town."

"Oh, I like college towns. They have lots of pretty girls."

"Pig!"

"Oink. Oink."

12

Danville, with its picture perfect main street, is home to Centre College, one of the top liberal arts colleges in the country. It is also called the "city of firsts," for it housed the first courthouse in Kentucky, the first post office west of the Allegheny Mountains, the first state-supported school for the deaf, and home to the first doctor, Ephraim McDowell, to successfully remove an ovarian tumor.

Ephraim McDowell was one of those doctors at the time that espoused cleanliness was next to godliness. In his outline for operations, he wrote that everything had to be "scrupulous clean." That was quite a novel thought at a time when doctors didn't even bother to wash their hands after seeing patients, let alone take a bath now and then.

Jane Todd Crawford, riding on horseback for sixty miles, came to see the good doctor. She had a serious medical problem. Her baby refused to be born and all seemed lost until she heard about this radical doctor in Danville.

Dr. McDowell confirmed that it was not a baby, but an ovarian tumor. He told the poor woman that she would die if not treated, but then again she would probably die when treated because he proposed to do something daring—cut into her body and remove the tumor. It was her decision.

Being a woman of grit, Mrs. Crawford agreed to the operation. On Christmas morning in 1809, without benefit of anesthetic or antisepsis, Ephraim McDowell cut into the pink flesh of Mrs. Crawford.

It is quite probable that she might have had a swig of whiskey before biting down on a leather strap to ease the pain. Nothing else was available.

The operation took an agonizing twenty-five minutes to remove a twenty-two pound tumor, but Mrs. Crawford survived to live another thirty years.

When Ephraim McDowell released his paper on the operation and his techniques, he was ridiculed by the medical profession.

It wasn't until he had an impressive list of surviving patients that other doctors started thinking that they too might have more surviving patients if they embraced the notion of cleanliness.

What a novel breakthrough!

Neff spotted the college's library and pulled the Avanti over. While Neff waited with the car, which was causing some excitement among students passing by, I ventured into the library. Seeing the front desk, I hurried over.

"Excuse me. Can you direct me to last week's Sunday paper?" I asked a young clerk.

"You can look on the computer if you have a card, but we don't keep the actual papers after a time. Are you a student here or live in the county?" she asked, smiling.

"No."

"Then I'm sorry. I can't give you a loaner's card."

"Are you sure you don't have the actual paper lying around somewhere?"

"Hold on for just a moment, please." She called someone on the phone and had a lengthy talk. "The building manager still has a copy in his office. He's bringing it right up for you."

"Thank you very much. That's very kind."

"My pleasure," responded the young clerk. "You can wait over there if you like," she suggested, pointing to a group of chairs.

The building manager soon found me and handed over a disarrayed paper. "Is this what you want, lady?"

"Yes, thank you very much. If you can direct me to some copy machines, I will give your paper back to you in a jiffy."

The man pointed toward the copy machines. I found

the lotto numbers and made three copies before handing the Sunday paper back.

Quickly I compared the numbers to the scrap of paper Ethel had given Neff. The numbers were not the same. Ethel's numbers hadn't won.

But since Suzy had told me that Jubal had not used Ethel's regular numbers, there was a chance that her lotto ticket still held the same numbers as the winning lot.

We had to find that lottery ticket and fast.

13

I called Merlene Crouch from my cell phone in the Avanti. Could we see her, as she was Miss Ethel's housekeeper?

After a few seconds of hesitation, Merlene agreed and gave me directions. We had to double back and drive to a potholed lane in Perryville.

"What a dump," belittled Neff.

"Shush. She might hear you." Silently I had to agree that the white clapboard house had seen better days. The left side of the house was sagging and desperately in need of paint. The windows were dirty plus some of the panes were broken and fixed with cardboard. The yard could have used a good cleaning as well.

"What? She probably knows she lives in a dump too."

Shaking my head, I knocked on the sagging front door.

A heavy woman in her late fifties answered the door. The left side of her face sagged a little like the house. I strongly suspected she had had a stroke and her face had never recovered fully.

"Hi. I'm Josiah Reynolds and this is Walter Neff. Mr. Neff is a private investigator working for Ethel Bradley. We understand that you work for her. May we talk to you? We won't take up too much of your time."

The woman stared at us with brown bloodshot eyes. There were dark circles under them.

"Are you Merlene Crouch?" I asked, not sure if we were talking to the right person.

"Aye. I am," she said. She opened the door further. "Please come in." She showed us into an old fashioned parlor with a collection of pink milk glass in several curio cabinets. All of the furniture was dark, heavy Victorian.

She extended her hand to a lumpy velvet couch and several chairs.

"Thank you," I said. I took a chair, as it was a rocker, but it didn't rock.

"Would you like something to drink?"

"Whaddya have?" asked Neff.

"No thank you," I interrupted, talking over Neff. "We'll only be here a moment."

"I see." Merlene settled into another rocker. It worked correctly. "What do you want to ask me?"

"Miss Ethel said that you have worked for her a long time."

"That's right. It's been over fifteen years, I reckon."
Neff started to speak, but I beat him to it. "Since you
two have been friends for so long I'm sure Ethel has
confided to you that she thinks strange things have been
happening lately."

"We're not friends. I work for the lady. That's all.
She hasn't given me a raise in over five years. She don't
confide in me and I don't tell her my woes neither."

"Oh." I wasn't expecting hard feelings.

Neff gave a little snort.

Merlene snapped her head toward Neff.

Neff's grin immediately disappeared. He leaned
forward in his chair. "You know that Ethel plays the
lottery every week."

"Aye. Everyone knows that."

"She seems to be missing her last ticket. Do you know
anything about that?"

Merlene bristled. "I hope you're not accusing me of
somethin'. I'm a Christian woman. My people are
Mennonites. I don't steal."

"He wasn't accusing you of anything," I claimed. "Mr.
Neff just wanted to know if you knew anything about the
ticket, like does Ethel often misplace things? Could she
have put the ticket somewhere in the house?"

Merlene's shoulders relaxed but her eyes blazed at
Neff. "She's got a good memory, that one. Mrs. Bradley
always puts her tickets in her Bible. She doesn't deviate
from that."

"Always?" I asked.

"She's a woman with set habits."

"Miss Ethel thinks her house might have been searched. Would you have any suspicion as to who might have searched her house?"

Merlene gave a little laugh. "Have you met her nephew, Jubal Bradley? He's a rough one, that boy. She knows where to look when something goes awry." Merlene rocked a bit. "I have to speak the entire truth here."

Neff and I leaned forward. I'm sure our eyes were wide with expectation.

"He's a good one to cut the grass and keep the yard. He checks on that old woman every week and takes her to the doctor, grocery, what not. So I guess you can say his bad ways even out with the good Jubal does her."

We both slumped back in our chairs like someone had let the air out of us. We didn't want to hear about Jubal's good points. We wanted the dirt on him. We wanted juicy.

"Miss Ethel said she got food poisoning from drinking apple cider." Neff stated it as fact rather than a question.

"Aye."

"She says you threw it out."

"It was bad. Started fermenting." Merlene stared back at Neff, who was eyeballing her. I don't think she liked him, but then who did.

"How could you tell?"

"It smelled bad. You can just tell. No mystery there. She picked a bad batch. It happens."

Disappointed, I asked, "Anything else you might want to tell us?"

"Can't say that I do."

Neff butted in. "Do you have a key to Ethel Bradley's house?"

"Don't be daft, little man." Merlene rose, as did we. The interview was over.

14

Neff unlocked the back door of Ethel's house, then handed the keys back to me.

"Don't let her cat out," I reminded Neff as he opened the door.

"Here puddy cat. Here puddy cat. I think I see a puddy cat. I do. I do." Neff pointed to a large lump on the kitchen table that finally moved. "It's not a puddy cat. It's a mountain lion," Neff professed.

"Goodness, that's one of the biggest cats I've ever seen," I gushed. Going over to the table, I began scratching the behemoth behind the ears. His immediate response was a fit of purring as he flopped over, exposing his oversized white belly.

Neff poured some cat food in the cat's bowl and changed his water. "Quit playing with the cat and let's get searching," he yammered.

"I think his litter box needs to be changed."

"You change it."

"You're the employee. You change it."

"If you are so concerned about this cat's potty box, you fix it. I'm busy."

"Surely you don't want Miss Ethel coming home to a smelly house?"

"I'm not paid to handle cat turds."

"You just are a turd."

"What was that?"

"Nothing. I'll go find the litter box." I followed the smell to the mudroom off the kitchen. It didn't take me long to find it. Next to the freezer was a very messy kitty bathroom. Not knowing Ethel's kitty cleaning routine, I took the box outside and dumped the contents in some weeds. After hosing the box out, I reentered the house to find a very disturbed cat meowing as it followed me into the mudroom. Finding the litter, I poured some in generously as well as a layer of baking soda. "That should do it," I murmured to myself.

The tabby cautiously sniffed at the box and then stepped in, giving it a try. "Well, that seems to do the job," I remarked, watching the cat use its bathroom. Happy that Petty was happy, I washed my hands and then went to find Neff.

"Any luck?" I asked.

Neff shook his head while thumbing through various magazines next to Ethel's TV chair. "I've already gone through the bedroom." He threw down the last magazine and pulled back the chair, checking underneath it. "Why don't you do the kitchen? Go through the freezer too. Make sure you unwrap everything."

"Okay. Don't forget to look under the furniture cushions."

Neff gave me an irritated look. "Does this look like my first rodeo? I know how to search a room."

"You don't have to get all huffy, Neff."

"Get lost!"

"Going, going, gone." I ventured into the kitchen. The tabby had finished his business and was now lounging back on the kitchen table licking his paws. I could not fathom how he jumped up with his weight.

I started with cookie jars. Ethel had quite a collection. Nothing. Next I checked through all the kitchen drawers. That didn't take very long. Nothing. Ethel was right when she asserted that she was a tidy person. I attacked the refrigerator and its freezer. Nothing again.

Getting tired, I pulled a chair over and then began going through the large freezer in the mudroom. I was halfway through when I felt something large looming over me.

I jerked my head around to see a huge man standing between the kitchen and me . . . and safety.

"Who the hell are you, lady?"

"Jumping Jehosaphat! You scared me."

"I'm gonna ask you again before I call the police. Who are you?"

Standing up, I stretched out my hand. "I'm Mrs. Reynolds. You must be Jubal Bradley, Ethel's nephew. She asked me to come and check on Petty. She was worried."

Jubal shifted his weight as he peered out from his green John Deere cap. "Why you going through her freezer? Looks like stealing to me." He didn't move to shake my hand.

I gave up a little hiccup of a nervous laugh. "She's staying with my neighbor, Lady Elsmere, and wanted to cook something special as a thank you for staying with her. You know Lady Elsmere? She lives on that big horse farm on Tates Creek."

"I know where she's staying. I talked to her this morning. She didn't say nothing about someone coming out and getting some meat for her."

"Maybe she thought of it after she talked to you. She wanted me to check on the cat too."

"You said that. You seem awful fidgety."

"Like I said, you frightened me."

"Hmmm," Jubal said, still giving me the once-over. "Somebody else with you?"

"Yes, my brother. He's checking the house for her."

"Hello. Someone call my name?" asked Neff, peeking into the kitchen. "Hello there. Are you Jubal? My name is Walter," announced Neff. "I see you've met my wife."

"Wife? She said you were her brother. What's going on here?"

"Did I say wife? I meant sister. My wife just left me and I keep thinking of her all the time. A Freudian slip. Come on, sis. Let's not bother this man anymore. I've got the yellow dress Ethel wanted. Did you get the roast?"

"Getting it now. Very nice to meet you, Jubal. I'll tell Ethel that you stopped by. You can lock up," I said, pushing by him. "Let's not keep Ethel waiting, brother." As I opened the back door, holding a very heavy roast I hesitated, "Oh, we fed the cat and cleaned his litter box."

Walter gave Jubal a wide smile while pushing me out the door before I could say anything else. We both ran to the car. Before I could throw the roast in the back seat or close my door, Neff was ramming the Avanti down the driveway.

When we were far enough away, Neff stopped at a gas station, buying two soft drinks.

I opened my bottle with haste.

"I always say women look dainty when chugging a sixteen ounce drink in ten seconds like a truck driver," sneered Neff.

"Do I laugh now or wait 'til you get funny?"

"You don't look very ladylike."

"I'm thirsty," I replied, wiping my chin with my hand.

"Obviously."

"Jubal is a really big man. Kinda scary."

"Yep, they don't make 'em like that anymore. Must have thyroid problems," Neff offered.

"Why was he there, you think?"

"To do the same that we were doing."

"Maybe he saw the car and came to investigate?" I responded.

"Nope. I parked way in the back. No one could see the car from the front road. He didn't know we were there until he came to the back of the house." And Neff concluded with a mischievous smile, "We closed the back door which automatically locks, which means Jubal must have had a key to unlock it."

"That's right," I realized with glee.

We clicked our soda pop bottles together.

One little mystery had been solved.

Jubal had a key to his aunt's house.

15

"I don't understand what you're trying to tell me," uttered Ethel, reaching for Lady Elsmere's hand. "Are you saying that Jubal searched my house?"

Neff threw his report on the table. "I'm saying that he has a key. That's why our search was cut short because he entered the house while we were there. He couldn't have done that if he hadn't had a copy of your key."

"Oh, dear," said Miss Ethel, looking bewildered. "Whatever shall I do then? He's my only kin."

"I am suggesting again that you install a security system with cameras."

"Miss Ethel, we didn't find your Bible. Do you know where it might be?" I asked, cutting in.

"It should have been on my bed stand. That's where I

always leave it except when I go to church."

"You don't read it in the living room or in the kitchen?" Neff questioned.

"No, just the bedroom. That way I always know where it is, you see."

"Do you have another Bible that you use sometimes?" asked Neff, unwrapping a piece of gum.

I made a face at him. Seeing my grimace, he reluctantly put the gum back in his pants pocket.

"No. Who would want my Bible?"

Silence permeated the room.

Finally Lady Elsmere spoke. "Ethel, you've got to face the fact that Jubal might be a rotten apple."

"He was always a hard-headed boy, and the years have not been good to him."

"Well, that's all I can do at the moment," explained Neff. "Take my advice–have the locks changed and put in a security system."

"Yes, I will, young man. Thank you for your help."

"Ummm, this is my invoice. Payment upon delivery."

Ethel perused the invoice like a squirrel judging a fat ear of corn. Finally, she came up for air. "I left my bag in the hallway. Will you fetch it for me?"

"You get it," Neff said to me. "I don't touch women's purses."

"All right," I fumed as I rose to get the handbag. "The sooner she writes her check, the sooner you get going."

"Baby, you're breaking my heart," kidded Neff. He

turned to Ethel and Lady Elsmere. "She loves me, but don't like to show her affection in front of folks."

"Doesn't," corrected Lady Elsmere.

"Huh?"

"Nothing." Lady Elsmere rolled her eyes.

The purse was on the sideboard in the main foyer along with Lady Elsmere's, which I had told and told her not to keep there, but would she listen?

I picked up Ethel's handbag. "Golly, this is heavy." I laid the purse back down on the sideboard and opened it. I'm such a stinker.

There was Ethel's Bible!

Hearing a sound, I turned. Behind me stood Giles with an accusing look on his face. "May I help you, Madam?"

Snapping the bag shut, I replied with as much dignity as possible, "No thank you," and sauntered around him.

Feeling Giles' reproving eyes upon my back, I hurried away. "I found your Bible, Ethel. It was in your purse."

"Really?" She eagerly pulled out the worn book.

"Open it," encouraged Neff.

"Well," demanded Lady Elsmere, leaning over to get a better view. "Is the ticket in there?"

"Give me a moment, June," protested Ethel. She carefully pulled out the lottery tickets that she used as bookmarks and handed them to me. "Check for me, dear. My hands are shaking too much."

I pulled out my newspaper copy of the lottery winners and checked the numbers against her tickets.

Neff stood behind looking over my shoulder. "Do you mind?" I snarled, shaking him off. "You're leaning on me."

"Sorry."

"The numbers don't match with Sunday's paper," I confirmed.

Ethel's face drooped. "I guess I didn't win."

"That's not necessarily so," assured Lady Elsmere. She turned to Neff. "Didn't you say in your report that the cashier said Jubal didn't play Ethel's regular numbers?"

"Yes. That's right."

Lady Elsmere took a sip of her whiskey sour before continuing. "Then you still might have won, Ethel. You've just got to remember where you put that last lottery ticket."

"June, I don't care anymore. I'm sick of the whole business. I just want to go home to Petty and forget this entire debacle. It's been most distressing."

"But Ethel, you just can't throw away a potential fortune," argued Lady Elsmere.

"If you don't mind, June, I don't want to talk about this anymore. I'm done with it." Standing up, she asked, "Young man, is our business concluded?"

"As far as I'm concerned. You got your report and I've got my money. Now this check won't bounce on me, will it?"

Ethel looked as though someone had thrown cold water in her face. "Of course not. What a thing to say." She angrily straightened her dress and picked up her purse. "June, thank you for everything, but tomorrow I'm going home."

"I wish you wouldn't, Ethel," lamented Lady Elsmere. "I've got a bad feeling. Nothing good is going to come of you going home before this is settled."

I sat watching everyone's expressions. I could tell Neff was thinking the same thing that I was—that Ethel had remembered what she had done with the lottery ticket and didn't want us to realize it.

I had a bad feeling too.

Nothing good was going to come of Ethel striking out on her own.

16

I was nervous. I was restless. I was shaky. I needed to unravel this puzzle. And when I needed to think, I visited my girls–the bees. Of course, at this time of the year the bees were tight in a cluster protecting the Queen, eating surplus honey and flexing their wings to keep the temperature warm.

There were almost no males in this harmonious group, as the drones were driven out or killed when the weather turned. They ate too much and were useless to the survival of the hive, so their sisters killed with impunity, knowing that their mother would lay more drone eggs in late winter when she starting gearing up the hive for the spring.

I could never stand to witness the expulsion of the drones. It was too cruel and I had had enough cruelty in my life, thank you. So when that process started, I would not visit the bee yard for days until I knew it was over.

Getting out of my golf cart, my thoughts reverted to Miss Ethel. I did not think the ending would bode well for Miss Ethel—not with millions of dollars at stake.

Jubal was not like the gentle drones in the hives, accepting their fate. He was faithful to no Queen and his male aggression was probably ramped up several notches by his gambling predicament and lust for the lottery winnings. From what Neff's report said of Jubal, he was one of those folks too poor to paint and too proud to whitewash. He saw the lottery ticket as his way out of a crippling lifestyle.

Thinking about Jubal and Ethel, I kneed the back of each hive. If the hive tilted forward easily, then it needed emergency feeding immediately. That was the first test.

After I inspected the food supplies, I surveyed the opening of each hive, making sure that it was clean and free of debris. If it was dirty with feces, then I knew the bees needed medicine as they had diarrhea, which would dehydrate them.

(Bees will break their cluster in order to fly out of the hive to go potty if the temperature is fifty degrees or higher. Sometimes I have seen them out at forty-five degrees. They are very clean insects).

Last but not least, I stood behind a hive and knocked loudly on its side. Then I listened to hear if the hive buzzed. If it did, then I knew that hive still had bees in it.

To my satisfaction, all the hives seemed in good condition, but one could never tell. I've opened up hives in the spring that were full of honey, free of disease, and dry. Not one bee in them.

Honeybees seemed to have a will of their own and do what they wished. They were unpredictable.

But it was the unpredictability of people that had me worried. Even being with my girls couldn't shake it. Something was not right.

It was as Shakespeare had written for me, "By the pricking of my thumbs, something wicked this way comes."

17

I was coming out of my audiologist's office when I glanced out of a window and chanced to see Meriah Caldwell get out of a cab and enter the building.

Jumping Jehosaphat! What was she doing back in town? And what was she doing at a doctor's building? I pushed the going-up button. If I were lucky to catch the elevator with Meriah on it, I could surprise her and find out what she was doing here.

Yes, I know it was none of my business.

To my luck, both of the elevators opened at the same time. Meriah was not on either of them, which meant she was on a lower floor. Behind me was a directory to the doctors' offices. I studied it with simple selfish curiosity.

First floor – Dermatology and Gastroenterology
Second floor – Pulmonary Diseases
Third floor – Obstetrics/Gynecology
Fourth floor – Cardiology

My eyes flew back to the third floor listing. Ob-Gyn. I slumped against the directory. It couldn't be. Could it? Determined to find out, I got on the elevator the next time it opened and pushed button three.

The door opened at level three where I tentatively stepped out. Slowly I walked around the hallways to find the entire floor consumed with doctors treating female complaints. Which office was she in?

The only way to know for sure was to enter each office and see if Meriah was sitting in the waiting room. Or I could wait outside at the main doorway and confront Meriah on the way out. That seemed the most fun– jumping out from behind a door and going "boo!" but not the most expedient. I could be waiting all day.

I started my campaign. I entered each office, sat down, picked up a magazine, and perused the room. Finding no Meriah, I would move on to the next office. I had to be unobtrusive, as I didn't want to be escorted out of the building by some roughneck security guards, but usually no one questions a woman who has a limp and a cane.

On my fourth try, I saw Meriah across the waiting room after I sat down. She was flipping through a magazine with restless, thin hands. In fact, she looked thinner than when I had last seen her, if that was possible, and had dark circles under her eyes.

Suddenly I felt ashamed of myself.

Here I was stalking Meriah when not even two months ago, a crazy woman had killed herself and another guest at Meriah's wedding. Meriah had fled to Los Angeles while I traveled to the east coast, both of us leaving Matt to deal with the aftermath.

Matt had told me that Meriah had not even said goodbye, but had left a note with Lady Elsmere saying that they were finished and she was never coming back.

Meriah must have been terribly frightened to do that, as I knew she loved Matt. Now here she was–looking unhappy and ill. I hoped nothing was seriously wrong, although I couldn't understand why she was seeing a doctor here and not in Los Angeles.

Matt would have told me if she were back . . . if he had known.

Picking up my purse, I began to make my way out of the waiting room when Meriah glanced up and recognized me. Her face drained of color as her eyes expressed both apprehension and confusion.

I felt like such a jerk. There was nothing to do now but say hello. "Meriah," I cooed. "This is something of an unexpected pleasure. I didn't know you were in town."

Meriah stared back with mistrust oozing from every pore. "I'm here for just a few days before I fly back," she finally coughed up. "And you are here why?"

"Oh, I'm here to get a pap smear," I lied. "Gotta get those done every year for women at my age."

"A pap smear, huh," parroted Meriah. "That's funny since this office specializes in obstetrics."

It hit me what she had said. "Meriah, are you? Is it Matt's?"

Meriah's face suddenly turned green as she grabbed at her belly. "I think I'm going to be sick." She rushed through a door that led to the examining rooms where the restrooms were located.

Several minutes later, an office clerk delivered a note to me.

On it was scrawled–"Get lost!"

I did.

18

In spite of Lady Elsmere's pleading, Ethel Bradley packed her overnight bag, determined to go home. Instead of letting Charles take her home, Ethel took a cab.

It took fifty minutes to get home. Ethel had to write a check for part of the fare, as it was more than the one hundred dollars she kept for emergencies.

The cabbie was not especially amused when she gave him a paltry three-dollar tip, but it was all the cash she had left in her handbag.

Grateful that she was home, Ethel unlocked the back door, breathing a sigh of relief. The house smelled clean.

That made Ethel feel better. She so liked to keep her house nice. She would have to write a thank you note to Josiah Reynolds for cleaning out Petty's litter box. "She didn't have to do that," Ethel muttered to herself, but was glad Josiah had.

Lady Elsmere's house was grand to be sure, but it wasn't home. Ethel could finally get a good night's sleep and drink tea out of her own china. Besides, she missed her tabby. "Petty. Petty," she called. "Petty! Now where is my precious?"

Ethel glanced in the living room. No cat on the couch. She pulled back the drapes from the bay window in the kitchen. No kitty hiding on the windowsill.

Hearing a faint meow, Ethel followed the sound and stepped into the mudroom off the kitchen. "Petty. Mommy's home, dearest."

Ethel found Petty all right.

At first she didn't notice Petty for the two men in her mudroom wearing ski masks. One of them was carrying Petty, who looked very, very unhappy.

Ethel didn't even think about screaming as she turned to run. She didn't get far.

Grabbing her from behind, the men roughly pushed her into a kitchen chair. Ethel gave a little cry when a burlap bag was pulled over her head.

Having been roughly dropped, Petty snuck under a pie safe, faintly meowing his distress.

"What did you do with that lottery ticket?" snarled one man in an obviously disguised voice.

Ethel wailed, "You didn't hurt my cat, did you? Petty? Petty?"

One of the men slapped the top of her head. "You better be worried about yourself instead of that stupid cat."

Startled at being struck, Ethel began to whimper. Her faded eyes filled with tears. Her chest felt tight. She started taking big gulps of air, but the bag over her head impeded her airflow.

"Where's the ticket?"

One of the thugs slammed his hand down on the kitchen table, causing the china in the cabinets to rattle.

Ethel flinched and made a little yelping noise.

"We want that ticket. Tell me or I'm gonna kill your cat, but first I'm gonna hurt him real bad. I'll start by breaking one leg at a time. Then we'll see how he likes burning matches. You wouldn't want to see your kitty suffer, would you? Tell me where the ticket is."

Blubbering, Ethel tried to get the words out but couldn't. She couldn't even catch her breath. Clutching at her chest, she gasped so loudly for air that she didn't hear Charles coming up the driveway, giving his car horn a quick honk.

But the hooded thugs did. They hightailed it out the back door, skedaddling through the back pasture to the woods. They were long gone before Charles entered the kitchen, but not before he caught sight of them running away.

19

"This is some mess," uttered Jubal in the emergency room

"Yes, isn't it," I replied. "It's a good thing Charles followed your aunt home. Who knows what would have happened if he hadn't come along."

"I appreciate you being here for my aunt. I know you must be tired, waiting for hours. I can take it from here."

"Yes, I am tired. Any idea who those men were?"

"None a'tall. My aunt doesn't have anything really valuable."

"It just seems like an awful lot of work for two men to mount a home invasion when the house has been empty for days."

"Maybe she surprised them."

"Then why were they wearing masks?"

Jubal shifted his weight. "You've talked to Ethel?"

"Just for a few seconds before they moved her to ICU."

"What else did she say?"

"We had the devil of a time trying to find you."

"I was at a bar and had turned off my cell phone."

"I see." Studying his boots and pants, I declared, "You must have been working outside this morning."

Jubal glanced at his muddy work boots and stained pants. "I was pulling out dead shrubbery around my house this morning. Ethel say anything else?"

"Like I said, just a few words to me."

"What about that guy who found her?"

"Charles? I don't think so. He told me she was having trouble breathing and couldn't speak at the time."

"Too bad she couldn't tell him more."

"Yes, too bad." I noticed Jubal's shirt had large sweat stains under his armpits. "Well, I'm going home. May I drop you off?" I asked.

"I think I'm gonna hang around and talk to the cops."

"They've already taken a report and left."

"Really? They have any clues?"

"If they did, they didn't confide in me."

"I think I'll stick around anyway. Ethel might need me."

"Will you please call Lady Elsmere if there is a change? She is worried sick and would be obliged for any news."

"Sure."

Somehow I didn't believe Jubal, but I left anyway. I was beat. It was late afternoon and I had been at the hospital for hours since Charles had called.

He was terribly upset at finding Ethel in her predicament and requested that I come. Charles was happy when I relieved him, so he could go home to Lady Elsmere, who was already drowning her concerns in mint juleps after hearing the news of her childhood friend. Only Charles could deal with June when she got this way.

But I didn't go straight home. I had a copy of Neff's report, which contained Jubal's address. Swinging by his house, I got out and walked its perimeter, looking for any evidence that Jubal had been working with shrubbery.

None.

I wouldn't have thought so. But a man could get his boots muddy and pants ruined by running through a pasture and then woods. There was no doubt in my mind that Jubal had been one of the men who had attacked Ethel.

But who was the other man? I doubt it would have been Jubal's loan shark. There was a hierarchy in threatening people relating to loan sharks. The loan shark would have directly threatened Jubal, not his aunt. So who was the other man?

Getting back in my car, I headed home. My left leg was beginning to throb and the sound was going out in my hearing aid again. I needed to replace its battery. Plus I was starving. Luckily for me, Eunice had been using my office to plan an upcoming reception at the Butterfly. I called and asked her to put something in the oven for me.

Getting home to the Butterfly in record time, I unlocked the door, punched in the security code for the alarm and then loved on Baby, who met me at the door. If Baby was happy, then I knew no one was in the house that he didn't like. My heart rate decreased automatically. Baby was my best security alarm.

"Josiah, is that you?" called Eunice from the office.

"Yes, Eunice. It's me."

"Did you put the alarm back on?"

"Doing it now."

"Dinner is in the oven. Should be done."

"Thanks. I just didn't have it in me to cook tonight," I announced.

"Salad in fridge."

"Okay. Got it." I pulled a small hot brown out of the oven and placed it on the polished limestone counter, letting it cool. An exquisite little garden salad waited for me in the fridge with Eunice's homemade ranch dressing, which I neatly folded in. I took both over to my Nakashima table that already had a place setting with a glass of water. I dove in, eating with relish. Nobody could make a hot brown like Eunice, not even me.

After eating, I took up residence on the couch over-looking the pool and the bird feeders. Baby laid down beside the couch and rested his big droopy head on his paws.

Cardinals, nut hatches, finches, downy woodpeckers, black-top chickadees, flickers, sparrows and rock doves crowded around the feeders in happy commotion.

Occasionally I would hear a sound from the office, but the house was quiet for the most part—just the humming of the refrigerator and the sound of air coming through the heat vents.

I didn't even notice when my head drooped over my chest and my eyes closed.

20

A banging on the door disturbed my sleep and then I heard the door unlock.

Still groggy, I slipped off the couch and rolled under it, which was stupid. Anyone could see a person hiding there, but it was the best I could think of still half asleep.

"Rennie! Rennie! Where are you?" yelled Matt. "Good God, what are you doing under the couch, woman?"

Thinking this a game, Baby stuck his snout under the couch and lunged.

"No, Baby. Bad Baby!" I admonished. I hated this game of his where he acted as though he was going to attack. I didn't like his lunging, especially around my face.

I guess we were going back to the dog trainer, as Baby was technically still a puppy—a huge, willful puppy.

Matt pulled Baby up by his collar and shook his finger at him. "Bad Baby. No."

I never thought shaking one's finger at Baby was a good idea since he might mistake it for a hotdog, but Matt could do as he pleased.

To my astonishment, Baby looked chastised and shuffled over to a chew toy.

Matt was now on his hands and knees trying to extract me from beneath the couch. Slowly we made headway.

"What were you doing?"

"I was asleep. I heard yelling and banging on the door. I was trying to hide. Guess it was instinct."

"It was a stupid place to hide."

"I didn't say it was smart, Matt. I said it was instinct. Why didn't you just call like a normal person?" I sputtered, putting my clothes to rights.

"I did. I called and called, but no one picked up. I knew you were at home. I thought something might have happened." Matt grabbed my arm. "Are you taking double doses of your pain medication? I know you went to see the doctor to have the prescription refilled."

I pulled away. "The battery's going out on my hearing aid."

"Josiah!" Matt scolded.

"I was too tired to replace it when I got home. That's why I didn't hear the phone."

"Can we argue about this later?"

"What did you want? You seem flustered."

"Your brain seems to be functioning at last. You're not drunk, are you?"

I made a face. "Ha ha."

"Guess who came to see me at work today?"

"Meriah," I retorted, without thinking.

"Jeez, you must have calluses from patting yourself on the back for being right all the time. I simply hate that."

"Was it Meriah?"

Matt pulled me down on the couch and held my hands. His blue eyes sparkled beneath long thick eyelashes.

"Matt, you're frightening me. Meriah's not going to die, is she?"

"Why would you say that?"

"No reason," I lied. "Why did she come to see you?"

"She's going to have a baby. My baby."

"Get out!"

"Can you believe it!"

"This is happy news, Matt?"

"Ecstatic. And the best part is she doesn't want to raise it. She wants to give me full custody."

"Slow down, Matt. Slow down. She doesn't want custody? What mother would give up her rights like that? That's not normal."

"Meriah said she realized that she's not cut out to be a full-time mother, plus she doesn't want the baby to grow up in Los Angeles. She will have visiting rights, but I will have full custody."

"I can't wrap my head around this."

"I spent all afternoon with her discussing the terms. Meriah will sign the custody papers as soon as they are drawn up."

I patted Matt's hands. "Be careful, Matt. This is a land mine."

"What's wrong?"

"Is Meriah having a hard pregnancy?"

"Yes, very difficult. In fact, she's coming here a month before the baby is due so she won't have to travel during the ninth month. She wants the baby to be born in Kentucky."

"Why can't you go out there?"

"She said she is going to need complete bed rest and quiet. She can't get that in Los Angeles with her friends calling all the time."

"Right now Meriah's in pain and frightened. This is not how she imagined her life would be at this point. She thought she'd be married and living the high life in Los Angeles, not alone and pregnant. She is doing what is logical in her mind, but when she sees her baby and holds it, the odds are that she will want to keep it."

"Then I'll make sure she signs the agreement before she leaves in a couple of days."

"Is that the way you want to treat someone you loved and were going to marry?"

Matt looked confused.

"Do you want to take Meriah to court if she changes her mind? Believe me, if you do, you will lose in the state of Kentucky. Judges always favor the biological mother. But most important, you will lose Meriah's goodwill and that, Matt, is precious.

"If you are hell bent on signing that agreement, do so, but tell Meriah that if she should change her mind, you will tear it up. Tell her that you love her and forgive her for leaving you. Give her peace of mind, Matt. That's why she came back."

Matt's face fell. "Don't you want me to have this baby? Don't you think I'll be a good father?"

"That's not it at all. You are going to be tied to Meriah the rest of your life because of this baby. You want to make it pleasant for both of you. Don't make the same mistakes that I did in my marriage by pushing an agenda all the time.

"Reassure her that whatever she wants, you'll do. If Meriah wants to sign away her rights, then let her do so, but assure her that if she changes her mind when the baby is born, you will work out an arrangement that you can both live with. Tell her everything will be alright."

Matt kissed my hand. "You're right. I'm seeing her again tomorrow. I will make sure she understands that we need to do what's best for the child, even if that means the child living with her. We'll work it out together."

"That's for the best, Matt. You won't be sorry."

"I want this baby, Rennie. Real bad."

"And most likely, Meriah will give you primary custody. I've always said women are like Thoroughbreds. Sometimes gentle treatment in the barn can do more for getting results than the whip on the track."

Matt pushed back his raven hair. "I guess I'll need to tell Franklin soon."

"You two an item again?"

"We have agreed to be friends. I still haven't decided how I want to live my life. He thinks I'm crazy, but we have agreed to see each other as compadres for now."

"Franklin agreed to that?"

"He is seeing a few people. You know . . . playing the field. Franklin will never be lonely. He has lots of friends. He's funny, charming, and smart. People like to be around him," Matt said.

"He's a bright light on a dull stage, that's for sure. And you are letting this funny, charming, and smart guy play the field while you change diapers?"

"You think I'm careless where Franklin is concerned."

"Franklin is a person of quality. He's a rare find. Don't think that you will find many more like him, because you won't."

"I'll tell Franklin about the baby after Meriah leaves. Until things are settled between us, there's no point involving him yet."

"Matt, let me tell Franklin. I think he can take the shock better hearing it from me rather than you."

"That's fine with me. But here you are comforting me and I never told you how sorry I was that Jake left."

Hearing Jake's name gave me a jolt . . . and not a pleasant one.

"He did the right thing. His kids needed him and so did his ex-wife."

"Miss him?"

When I didn't reply, Matt squeezed my hand.

I really wished he hadn't brought up Jake.

21

Franklin had a look of dread when he let me into his apartment, but he listened with quiet politeness as I explained the situation with Matt.

Then Franklin camped, "I need a stiff one, then maybe a drink."

I poured him bourbon.

Franklin held up the glass. "Here's to swimmin' with bow-legged women" and downed the entire drink. After wiping his mouth with his sleeve, he hiccupped and asked for another one.

"There's a limit to feeling sorry for yourself," I notified him.

"This from the queen of pity parties!" he retorted. "I guess it's finished with Matt. Over."

"Not necessarily. He's just having a baby. He's not madly in love with someone else."

"He's in love with Meriah."

"But I think Meriah realized that a long-term relationship with Matt was not in the cards or she wouldn't have left Kentucky after the wedding."

"I thought she was running from the blood that splattered over all her guests."

Ignoring his comment, I said, "As you recounted to Matt, he has no taste. He'll need help with decorating the nursery, picking out baby clothes, hiring a good nanny.

"Think of it if he has a baby girl. Do you want to see his baby paraded around town in hideous frocks by a frostbitten old nanny? That won't reflect well on you, Franklin—you being his friend. You've a reputation to uphold. Standards."

"Oh my gosh. We can be just like the couple in *Le Cage Au Folles.*" Franklin clapped his hands together at the thought of a baby. "Golly, I think my nipples are getting sore. I'm already lactating."

"See, that maternal instinct is kicking in."

"What should I do?"

"Congratulate Matt on his impending fatherhood and offer to help him. I don't think he'll turn you down. He hasn't a clue what to do."

"And he'll need help when the baby comes."

"Lots of it, because I won't be babysitting," I claimed. "I love babies."

"I could barely stand my own child, let alone other people's children. Sorry, but I agree with Stephen King–'Schizoid behavior is a pretty common thing in children. It's accepted, because all we adults have this unspoken agreement that children are lunatics.'"

"Philistine."

"Matt's waiting at his bungalow if you want to see him."

"Tell him I'll be there after I get my tape measure and color samples."

"I'll let myself out."

But Franklin didn't hear me, as he was already dashing about gathering things he would need to make Matt's spare bedroom into a nursery.

I hoped things worked out for Matt and Franklin. They deserved to find some happiness in this world.

Looking at my watch, I had just enough time.

Ethel's church would soon be letting out for its Saturday night service.

22

After parking my car in the back of the church, I let myself in the basement door. There I pulled out a flashlight and followed the instructions written on the church's stationary. Finding the custodian's closet, I sat inside on a chair that had been placed for me. Now all I had to do was wait.

I heard the last hymn, the pastor discharging the congregation, the stamping of feet in the aisles, the calls of goodbyes amongst friends, volunteers straightening up the sanctuary, and finally silence. Dull silence.

Bored, I found bottles of grape juice the church used for communion. I thought about it for a . . . oh, nano second . . . and then I drank most of it.

I told you I was a sinner.

A half-hour later, there was the subtle creaking of footfalls on the ancient wooden floor above. It was time to make my move.

Creeping up the staircase in the dark, I felt along the wall until I came to a fuse box. Beyond that was the master light switch for the entire church. I counted each lever and finally pulled the third one down. Immediately all the lights in the sanctuary came on.

I stepped inside the sanctuary and pulled out a gun from my coat pocket. "Hello," I uttered. "I knew it would be you."

There stood Walter Neff, holding a tiny flashlight in his mouth, going through each hymnal looking for the lottery ticket. "This isn't what it looks like, Toots," he sputtered after spitting out the flashlight.

"Yes, it is. I knew that you would be here at the first opportunity because you had figured out where Ethel might have put that lottery ticket."

"Aw, come on. It's me. I'm just doing my job looking out for Miss Ethel." He began creeping toward me.

"Stop right there, Walter. I'm warning you."

Walter stopped with a greasy smile fixed on his face. "What do you think you know?"

"It was you and Jubal who attacked Ethel, but that didn't work out so well, did it?"

"I guess we applied a little too much pressure. Is she okay?"

"Barely, thanks to you two. It was quite a shock for her."

"How was I to know that a little excitement would be too much for the old gal?"

"It's not customary for ladies in their eighties to be manhandled, especially by their relatives and men they hire to protect their interests. Shame on you, Walter. That was very naughty. I'm pretty sure that type of behavior is not in the shamus book of rules and customer etiquette."

"I didn't slap her or nothing. Just put a bag over her head. Didn't even hurt that old mangy cat of hers. Just threatened. See?"

"Unhuh."

"What gave me away?"

"I knew Jubal was one of the intruders. It was his clothes. His pants were stained and his boots were dirty when he came to the hospital. Charles told me that the two men ran through the fields. If Charles hadn't seen that, then you and Jubal might have gotten away with it for some time, but I would have figured it out soon or later."

"But why me?"

"It was only logical that the other man was you."

"Why?"

"Because you were in the room when Ethel suddenly decided to go home. When she made that fuss that she wanted to go home, your body language changed. You tensed up."

"That's 'cause I was next to you. Come on. You feel

the tension between us. I bet you're fire between the sheets. Your type always is."

I continued. "You're perceptive, just like me. We both figured that Ethel had finally remembered where she might have placed that ticket. That's why she was so agitated."

"So what."

"I think it went like this. You went to Jubal, threatening him that you would tell Ethel he was the one who sabotaged her brake line. She would have cut all ties with him and removed him from her will. Jubal couldn't have that, so he made a deal with you. What was it? Thirty percent, forty?"

"Fifty. I told him that I believed I knew where the ticket was and for my share of the loot, I would keep quiet."

"Blackmail. Tsk. Tsk."

"Blackmail is such an ugly word. I prefer to call it a business arrangement. How did you guess where the ticket was?"

"I figured that you and Jubal had combed Ethel's house and car. You wouldn't have attacked her if you had found it."

"Not attacked. Interviewed. We just put the bag over Ethel's head to frighten her a bit. We never planned to go farther. I swear it. We never meant to hurt that old biddy."

"The only other place that Ethel went on a regular basis was church."

"Ain't you gonna listen to me, Josiah? I deserve a break here. Come on now, Toots. Listen to me. Would you just shut up for a moment?"

I kept rattling on. "It would make sense that perhaps she used the tickets as bookmarks in hymnals as she did in her Bible.

"But you couldn't break into the church. If you got caught, you would have no explanation of why you were here and you needed lots of time to examine all the hymnals. So you waited for the next church service and, posing as a visitor, hid in the men's bathroom until everyone had left. That would give you all night to search if you had to."

"But then you just had to drop by and spoil my fun. Come on, Josiah. Let's make a deal. I know you could use the money. I'll give you ten percent of my half. No? Okay. Twenty-five." He inched toward me.

"I'm warning you not to move again, Walter. I don't want to shoot you, but I will."

"No you won't. You'll take the deal. Ethel's old. She's just gonna throw those cool greenbacks away on a bunch of nobodies. She doesn't need the money, but you do. Your part will be millions. No one will know. Your reputation will be safe.

"You can hobnob with your rich friends again, without feeling like the redheaded stepchild. Ain't you tired of being poor?" Walter continued inching his way toward me. "You and I could go far. We're both smart, savvy. With that money pooled together, we could do a lot for each other . . . for this community. You'd like that, wouldn't you? We could set up a foundation. We could run this town together, you and me. Only we give the money away to people who count. You could be important, like you used to be."

"What do you want me to say? Okay, Walter. Just as you want it. Straight down the line."

"What's wrong with that?"

"You forget one thing, Walter. You weren't picked because you're so darn smart. You're just a shade less dumb than the rest of the private dicks out there."

"I'm smarter than you, Toots. I've always been a step ahead."

"You're dumber, Walter. And shorter. I never did cotton to short men."

Walter laughed. "Sure, Toots. Whatever you say."

"I mean it. A smart person would have called Ethel's pastor and confirmed that Ethel sits in the same pew every Sunday. I figured she would. Old people usually keep the same routines.

"If you had been smart, you would have called to ask the pastor the same thing, still pretending to work for Ethel. But you didn't think of it which is why I have the lottery ticket."

"You what?"

"I came this afternoon and met with the pastor, explaining the situation. We went to Ethel's regular seat and checked the two hymnals stationed there. In the second one, I found this."

I pulled a lottery ticket out of my coat pocket.

"You're lying. It's a fake you've got there."

"I assure you, Walter, it is the real deal."

"Give it to me!" snarled Walter, his face a mask of fury. "Give it to me or I'll kill you with my bare hands!"

"I don't think so."

"You're rotten," cried Walter as he lunged for me.

"You're rottener," I spat out as I pulled the trigger.

23

Don't get your panties in a wad.

I didn't kill him.

I shot him with my stun gun.

He had a nasty headache and some burn marks.

The ER nurse called the cops, but Walter and I concocted a fake story that Walter had been examining the gun when he accidentally pulled the trigger.

Walter had a hell of a headache for several days.

Why didn't I tell the cop the real story?

Ethel couldn't have stood the attention that the story

would have garnered. She was of the old-fashioned belief that a lady's name should only be in the paper to announce her engagement of marriage and then her death. No. No. Publicity was out of the question.

Besides, the pastor and several church members had been in the choir loft upstairs taping the entire conversation. He and his deacons read the riot act to both Walter, and later Jubal, to stay away from Ethel or else they would turn the tape over to the authorities.

Both Walter and Jubal were neutered, if you wish to use that term. I certainly like it.

You lose some. You win some.

Walter just happened to lose that time.

It wasn't that Walter didn't play it smart.

I just played it smarter.

24

All of the accused were seated, with Lady Elsmere perched in an overstuffed chair that resembled a throne. And as any queen, she was going to pronounce judgment.

I sat a little behind her, being there mainly for support. Nobody maintained eye contact with either Lady Elsmere or me, but looked out the window, at their shoestrings or their fingernails, suddenly discovering that they needed cleaning.

There was Charles and his wife, their daughters and the grandsons. Also sitting was Mike Connor, who kept glancing at the liquor cabinet. Beside him sat Giles tugging at his shirt collar. Then there was Sir Anthony, looking quite miffed that the help was allowed to sit.

Lady Elsmere calmly looked around the room and felt a keen sense of delight that she could still cause people to pee in their pants. Not literally, of course.

"It seems that I have caused pandemonium when I wished for harmony by trying to please everyone. And a person can't please everyone." She twisted in her seat to look at me. "Josiah, what was that Lincoln said about pleasing people?"

"He said, 'You can please some of the people all of the time, all of the people some of the time, but you can never please all of the people all of the time.'"

"Exactly. I should have followed such sound advice. By not doing so, I have divided my own house. So the boom is going to be lowered and things set back to right. There will be no fussing or groaning. Do I make myself clear?"

Sir Anthony started to speak, but Lady Elsmere cut him off. "Don't speak, Tony. I think it would be your undoing."

Thinking better of it, Tony clammed shut. Seeing that he was outgunned, he began picking lint off his trousers.

"Charles," began Lady Elsmere, "I thought I was doing the right thing by making you take over the farm, but I see now that is not where your talents lie. So starting today, you will move out of the main house into your little cottage and take over your regular duties. I was trying to incorporate you early into the Big House, but I understand that it made you and your family uncomfortable. When I die, you may choose to live here or not. That is up to you, but I hope you do. This house needs a master.

"I want to assure you that you remain my heir and the will is airtight. I have made sure of it."

Charles nodded.

I could tell that he was relieved.

"Mr. Connor."

"Yes, ma'am."

"You are to oversee the running and maintaining of the farm and its livestock under my jurisdiction and then for Charles after my death. I better have a Derby winner before I die."

With a huge grin on his face, Mike leapt to his feet. "You can count on that."

"Better hurry," quipped Sir Anthony.

"What was that, Tony?" asked Lady Elsmere.

"Nothing, Aunt."

"Thought so.

"I'll do you right, Miss June," promised Mike.

Sir Anthony rolled his eyes. "She should be addressed as Lady Elsmere. Really."

"Mike. Charles. You all can leave. Tony—you stay with your man."

The DuPuys quickly left the room behind Mike and shut the door quietly, but I had no doubt that they were listening and peeking through the keyhole.

"Tony, I have never liked the British system of allocating everything to one heir. I know they do it to keep the estates and wealth intact, but frankly, when there is an heir and a spare–the spare is a pain in everyone's arse. And you have become a great pain in my backside."

"I resent that implication."

"Oh, shut up. The game is over. Now I don't blame you entirely. When one is raised as a wealthy brat, that brat assumes that will always be his station in life, but then the older brother gets the estate and the little brother is thrown out on his keister."

I was hoping that June would soon refrain from making allusions to one's buttocks. I didn't like where it was making me look.

"I have talked to your brother and convinced him that it is wrong to deny you part of your father's fortune, so he is going to settle two and a half million pounds on you, to be paid in installments every year until your death or it is paid out. I am going to settle three million U.S. dollars on you now. Here is the check." She handed Sir Anthony the check.

"Now, that won't make you fabulously rich, but it will keep up appearances so that you can hobnob with your friends and not have them make snobby comments behind your back."

"I don't know what to say, Aunt," Tony said, his lips quivering.

"You should thank Charles, as he agreed to let go of some of his inheritance to make a settlement on you. Tony, don't go yet. I'm not finished. You may live here as long as you like, but you are never to make trouble for Charles and his family again."

"I don't know what you mean?"

Lady Elsmere smiled and pulled a pocket watch out of the folds of her skirt. "I believe this belongs to you."

"My antique pocket watch. Where did you find it?"

"Where you had your man, Giles, put it–in Amelia's room. She gave it to Josiah last week after she discovered it in a shoebox." Lady Elsmere gave Tony a wicked smile. "We colonists are not the idiots you take us for. Josiah called her daughter to do a background check on you and your man. We found out that Giles is not really Giles, a gentleman's valet, but Liam Doyle. He is what we call, here in the states, a grifter."

Giles made a run for the door but found that it was locked.

"Hey, what goes on here?" sputtered Giles.

"Calm down," cautioned Lady Elsmere. "No one is going to call the police. If you wish, you may stay as Sir Anthony's valet, but you are to leave your wicked ways outside the door. That is, unless I need you to do something for me."

"Blackmail is it then?" Giles, aka Liam Doyle, accused.

"What an excitable little man you are. You can try your luck elsewhere."

"Just the occasional odd job?"

Lady Elsmere tilted her head. "Well, here you eat steak, but you're welcome to eat baloney elsewhere."

"I won't kill nobody. I won't!"

"You silly little man. No one is going to ask you to murder. Get out. Have a cup of tea to settle your nerves."

Lady Elsmere picked up the phone and called on the servant's line. "Charles, you can unlock the door now. And Charles? Will you be serving dinner tonight? That sounds grand." She put down the phone, smiling. "No more bickering. Back to normal."

"Are you finished with me, Aunt?"

"Are you staying, Tony? You may find a rich widow to marry. Who knows what the future may bring."

"I think for awhile. At least till I get my bearings." He looked down at the check. "Thanks for everything."

"That's what family is for. Now put it in the bank. Don't gamble it away because there won't be a second chance."

He nodded and followed Giles out of the room. I heard Giles, in the hallway, asking for his wages, which apparently hadn't been paid in quite some time.

Lady Elsmere poured herself a whiskey. "Want one, Josiah? How do you think that went?"

"The world is back in balance."

"You know what makes me so damned mad? I don't want to die. I'm having much too much fun, but this body is giving out. I'm just wise enough now to know how to be happy. Ain't that a kick in the pants!"

I accepted a glass of whiskey. There was that butt allusion again. "Here's to your health, June."

"And to yours, my dear friend."

25

Walter Neff was nursing a drink at Al's Bar on Sixth and Limestone. He intended to do more than nurse it. He was going to get stinking drunk.

Neff was bitter. He was bitter because he had been cheated out of millions by a dame he liked. It was hard to lose the money, but the money and the woman both? It made him feel like a worthless chump. Neff just hated to come up empty.

His mind raced with a thousand schemes. The money was lost, but maybe he could still have the dame. It was worth a shot.

Anger and jealousy gnawed at him. He knew deep in his heart that the woman was out of his reach.

Neff slammed the bar countertop in frustration with his fist.

"Whoa there, partner," drawled a handsome blond-haired man. He looked like Tab Hunter. "Got problems?"

"None of your business, pard-nar," sneered Neff.

"That's where you're wrong, partner."

Neff turned to get a good look at his companion. "What makes you say so?"

"I would say that we have mutual friends. Perhaps mutual experiences as well?"

"Sure we do, buddy." Neff turned back on his stool and took another sip of his drink.

The blond man leaned in closer. "I'm very serious. I'm always serious with people who have been burned by a certain redhead."

Neff faced the younger man and wavered for a moment. "Okay. I'll throw caution to the wind. What's your pitch?"

"I know that a woman with red hair and green eyes cost you millions of dollars. Money that is now being wasted on Lexington's terminally down and out."

"How do you know that?"

"I make it my business to know. Let's just say I've had previous experiences with the lady in question."

Neff squinted while tapping his forehead. His mind was fuzzy, but still worked when he concentrated. "I know who you are. You're that loser that went crazy and tried to . . ."

"If I'm a loser, so are you. Perhaps you would like to discuss how to become a winner. I have a plan. Would you like to hear it?"

Neff hesitated for a moment, but his anger was stronger that his common sense. "Let's talk where there ain't so many ears."

"That's all right with me. By the way, my name is O'nan. Fred O'nan."

Neff shook his hand. "I have the feeling that this is the beginning of a beautiful friendship."

"So do I," cooed O'nan, studying Neff like a wildcat does a careless rabbit. "So do I."

26

In a corner booth sat a young woman with short ash blond hair. She was preening in a compact mirror while powdering her nose, which drew attention from her gadget resembling a smart phone taping O'nan and Neff.

When O'nan and Neff left the bar together, the woman nodded to two men sitting at the bar.

Taking their cue, they sauntered out of the bar following the pair.

Another man immediately scooted into the booth with the woman. "Put eyes and ears in both their apartments. I want each room available. Make sure you tag their cars as well."

"Sure thing, Asa. Cars are already booted," he said in a cockney accent.

Asa frowned at the use of her name. Her tone turned very chilly. "I want their every movement tracked."

Getting the message, the man reminded her, "This is gonna cost a bundle."

"Don't worry about the money. I will take care of everyone. Just do your best."

"Yes, ma'am."

"You've seen O'nan's psychological profile. If it were your mother, what would you do?"

"He would have already been neutralized. Made it look like a car accident . . . if he had been bothering me mum, ma'am."

Asa nodded in agreement. She wasn't ruling that option out.

She threw a twenty on the table and left with her employee. Outside they parted. Asa got into a black SUV with government tags and pulled off her wig. "Take me home," she said to the driver.

"To the airport?"

"Sorry, no. Take me home to the Butterfly. I need to see my mother."

Before the SUV could take off, the back door was wrenched open.

"What are you doing here, Asa?" asked Officer Kelly, leaning in. "I was sitting in the back watching you watching O'nan. Don't do anything stupid. The city

would love to see your mother trip up so they don't have
to pay her the rest of the settlement. And don't think
they don't know you're here. There were three other
cops at Al's Bar tonight."

"I must be getting sloppy," admitted Asa. She smiled
sweetly at him.

Kelly's eyes grew soft. "Asa. Asa."

Asa leaned forward and kissed Kelly, holding onto him
tightly.

He passionately returned her kiss, winding his arms
about her. Asa pulled Kelly into the back seat and
mouthed to her driver–GO!

"Where're we going?" asked a bewildered Kelly.

"Shut up," replied Asa tenderly. "Just shut up and kiss
me."

Epilogue

The story has a happy ending. Ethel's pastor redeemed the lottery ticket on her behalf. When the money came through, Ethel immediately threw ten thousand at Jubal, and put in her will that he was to receive two million after her "natural death."

I never told Ethel that her only living kin had tried to harm her. Jubal would never be a problem to Ethel again–not with the deacons from Ethel's church looking on. There was no point in destroying their relationship. Let sleeping dogs lie, I say.

I'm not a fan of total honesty. There is no point in telling a woman who's in love with a new dress that she looks hideous in it. She will never forgive you for that honest review. I wish I had kept my mouth shut more during my marriage. If I'd had that philosophy then, I might have kept my husband.

Just a little side note—two days after Jubal received his ten thousand dollars, he got drunk as a skunk and crashed his car into a hundred-year-old white oak tree on Posey Ridge Road. He arrived at the hospital D.O.A. Poor greedy Jubal.

"That's a bright spot," declared Lady Elsmere upon hearing the news. "I never liked the man. He was always a cheat."

I concurred. "She's better off without him mudding up the works."

After Jubal's funeral, Ethel gave her church a spanking new roof, a new furnace, new paint job, and fancy cushioned pews.

The rest of the lottery money was given to the church in the name of Ethel's deceased husband and son as an endowment to do "good deeds" regardless of race, creed, or religion. Just heal the sick and feed the hungry like in the Good Book. Ethel's pastor became her adopted son and took wonderful care of her. She and Petty lived another five years in happy contentment. When Petty died, Ethel followed her beloved tabby two days later. They were buried together.

When the pastor inherited Jubal's two million, he donated half of it to his church so that Ethel's money would continue to do "good deeds" for a long time.

Then the pastor gave his two weeks notice to the church board. With his other million safely tucked away in a bank in the Bahamas, he tipped his hat, waved goodbye, and retired to some tropical island, never to step inside a church again.

Walter Neff continues to work as a shamus. He crosses the street when he sees me. Walter should have been more of a stand-up guy.

Like I said—you win some. You lose some.

BONUS CHAPTERS

DEATH BY CHOCOLATE
A Josiah Reynolds Mystery

&

LAST CHANCE MOTEL
A Last Chance For Love Romance Novel

Prologue

Linc and I were chopping nuts for Thanksgiving when someone began banging the front door and ringing the doorbell.

My heart jumped into my throat. I told Linc to take Baby and go into my bedroom, locking the steel door. He was not to come out until his grandmother told him it was okay.

Linc, thrilled at the prospect of danger, did what he was told.

So did Baby, who was thrilled at the prospect of being alone with Linc, who fascinated him. I think Baby thought Linc was his pet.

I had had several panic buttons installed in the house and was sitting next to one, ready to press, when Eunice exclaimed, "Why it's Ginny Wheelwright! She looks fit to be tied. You want me to tell her you're home?"

"She must have news about her boy," I replied. "Let her in, by all means."

Eunice barely opened the front door when Ginny swept passed her.

"Josiah. Josiah!" she called, looking in the kitchen.

"I'm over here."

Ginny looked a mess. Her face was blotchy and her one good eye was red from crying. To make her look totally alien, her glass eye had flipped over, showing only the gold side, but then would flip again when she twitched.

I guess my face showed my astonishment at her appearance.

"I know I look a mess. Can't help that now."

"Ginny. They've found Dwight's body?"

"If only. That would give me some peace on the matter. Oh, Josiah. That wife of his has petitioned to have Dwight declared dead."

"You have to be missing seven years in order to be declared dead."

"That's what I thought, but if she can prove extenuating circumstances, then the court will give an earlier approval."

"What's the rush? Dwight's only been gone five months. Give the detectives a little longer to work the case. Dwight might be stumbling around somewhere with amnesia. It's been known to happen."

"That's what I said, but she said she wanted to get on with her life."

"Her childhood sweetheart goes missing for only five months and she wants to forget about him?"

"My sentiments, exactly. I think it's awfully cold of her."

"What else did she say?"

"She told me to mind my own business." Ginny began crying. "My son is my business. Where is he, Josiah? Where can my baby be?"

Eunice brought a tray of coffee, tea, cookies, and a box of tissues. Then she discreetly vamoosed into my office, giving Ginny some privacy.

I'm not a touchy-feely person. I'm not given to hugs or kisses, but I did reach out and pat Ginny's hand.

Ginny grabbed it and tugged. "Ya gotta help me, Jo. The investigation is going nowhere."

Shaking my head, I said, "NOOO. I'm not going to get involved with issues like this anymore."

"This isn't some issue. This is my boy who used to play with your girl right there on that patio. You babysat him. You cooked for him."

I tried to pull away.

"When Asa went to trial, who was there for you? Me. When Brannon left, so did most of your friends, but I stuck by you. Now it's payback time. You gotta help me."

Jumping Jehosaphat! Why did I have to stick my hand out to her? I was in no shape physically or emotionally to solve another mystery. That's what police and shamuses were for. I should have thrown Ginny out right then and there.

Instead, I asked, "What do you want me to do?"

Last Chance Motel
A Romance Novel

Eva gazed into the floor-length mirror and was pleased with her reflection. The black negligee she had recently purchased encased her trim body like a glove. Her auburn hair glimmered with highlights and her skin looked like butter cream. Even though she was forty, Eva looked younger and worked at it.

Hoping that her sexy look might heat up her husband, who seemed a little frost-bitten lately, she put on the finishing touch. Passion Fire Red lipstick!

Nine years ago, she had met Dennis while helping his company remodel an old warehouse on the west side of Manhattan. Her boss had put Eva in charge of the cosmetic rehab of the warehouse while others dealt with structural issues. That was okay with Eva. Buying furniture and picking out paint colors was fun and she was given a huge budget with which to play.

It was at a briefing that Eva was introduced to Dennis, a junior executive at that time. He was to be the company's liaison with her.

There was instant chemistry and before long they were embroiled in a passionate affair, which spilled over into marriage two months after the project was completed.

Nine years. Eva shook her head in disbelief. Where had the time gone? Six of those years had been fantastic, but things started slipping three years ago.

It had begun when Eva and Dennis purchased an abandoned brownstone in Brooklyn near the Verrazano Bridge. They had been giddy when they first received the keys from the bank and began restoring the four-story brownstone, but things started taking a downward turn six months into the project.

To save money, Eva and Dennis decided to complete many of the cosmetic projects themselves. After working long hours at their firms, they would hurry home to the brownstone and work late into the night trying to tile the bathrooms or lay down bamboo floors or paint twelve foot ceilings. What started as fun became a strain both physically and mentally.

They began snapping at each other and it didn't take long to realize that they both had different visions for the brownstone, which created even more tension.

Eva wanted to restore the brownstone to its authentic former glory while Dennis wanted to gut and modernize it completely.

Dennis won.

When the brownstone was completed, Eva had to admit it was stunning, complete with all modern amenities. But to Eva, the brownstone was cold and void of any personality, but it was what Dennis liked. She disliked the cold paint colors he had chosen and the minimalist look of each room.

Eva realized that compromise was the cornerstone of marriage and wanted Dennis to be happy. That was very important to her. She could live with the renovation.

Now that the brownstone was finished, Eva wanted to heat up her faltering relationship with her husband and get it back on track.

Eva masked her irritation when Dennis finally got home . . . late as usual during the past seven months. Hearing the elevator rise to the master bedroom floor, Eva waited in the alcove trying to look sexy in her negligee.

The elevator reached the top and the door swung open. Dennis was going through the mail and barely looked up.

"Hello there, big boy," teased Eva.

Dennis looked up and froze when he saw Eva.

Eva noticed his hesitation and it threw her off her game. She suddenly felt foolish.

"What's up with you?" asked Dennis.

Eva, determined that the night be a success, smiled. "I thought we would celebrate your new promotion and the completion of the house. I have made a very nice dinner for us and then for dessert . . ."

"We celebrated last Saturday with our friends," retorted Dennis. He looked frustrated and a bit embarrassed.

"Yes, but I thought we could have a private celebration, just you and me," rejoined Eva.

Uh oh. This was not going as planned.

"Honey, I'm tired. I just want to eat and go to bed."

"Long day at the office?"

Dennis looked at the letters in his hand. His face was flushed. "Something like that."

"I have something that will make you feel better," chirped Eva. She was going to hit this out of the ballpark. Eva handed him two airline tickets.

"What's this?" Dennis asked, staring blankly at the tickets.

"I purchased two tickets to Miami for this weekend. The two of us on a getaway. No work. No house to think about. Just warm breezes and blue water. We can rent a boat and . . ."

"NO!"

"No?" echoed Eva. Her heart began to sink. Something was very wrong.

"This has got to end," Dennis said, cutting in, letting the mail fall to the floor. He looked at Eva as though he was looking through her. "I'm sorry I have let this go on for so long, but things have got to change."

Alarmed, Eva tried to hug Dennis but he pushed her away. Eva gasped. "What is it, Dennis? What's wrong? Are you ill?" She felt a numbing fear move up her spine.

"I'm sorry, Eva, but I'm not going anywhere with you. This is very hard to say but I . . . I want a divorce."

Eva felt like a bullet had passed through her. "What? For heaven's sake, why? We have everything. We worked so hard on this house. Why Dennis? Why?"

"I don't love you anymore. That's why."

2

"Mr. Reardon wants the brownstone," demanded Dennis' lawyer.

Eva and her attorney sat across the conference table. "Where is Dennis?" Eva asked. Turning to her lawyer, she questioned, "Shouldn't Dennis be here?"

"Mr. Reardon has given me instructions to act on his behalf and feels his presence is not necessary under the circumstances."

"What circumstances? Not seeing me?" Eva asked.

"Eva," cautioned her lawyer. "Let me handle this."

"What circumstances are you referring to?" Eva asked again.

"I believe that Mr. Reardon has expressed concern about you being abusive lately."

Eva snorted in derision.

"Many women become upset when asked for a divorce and given no reason. Mrs. Reardon has been a faithful and constant companion to Mr. Reardon. I think that under the circumstances most women would raise their voices and maybe even throw some objects. It's human nature."

"Mr. Reardon feared for his life."

"Oh, please," scoffed Eva. "Give me a break."

"If Mr. Reardon feared for his safety he should have called the police and filed a complaint. Since there is no complaint, let's move on, shall we. Alleging that Mrs. Reardon is a threat without proof is counter-productive to your client's requests."

"Demands," rebuffed Dennis' lawyer.

"What are they?" asked Eva's attorney, putting a pencil to a legal pad.

"Quite simply, Mr. Reardon wants the brownstone." Dennis' attorney raised his hand. "I have been authorized to offer eight hundred thousand for your half, Mrs. Reardon, plus half of all moneyed accounts that you share with Mr. Reardon. I think it is a very equitable division of assets."

"I don't understand why Dennis would want the brownstone. It's too large for one person. I thought we were going to sell it and divide the proceeds," remarked Eva.

"They think that they . . ." the lawyer stopped suddenly, looking aghast at his faux pas.

"They?" questioned Eva.

"I meant he," stated Dennis' lawyer.

"You said 'they'."

Shaken, Eva leaned back in her seat. "They. That explains a lot. It's the missing piece of the puzzle of why he left me." She began to sob quietly.

Her lawyer closed his notebook. "Tell Mr. Reardon that Mrs. Reardon wants 1.2 million plus half of all the other assets or we are going to drag this out indefinitely."

"Oh no, you can't do that," complained Dennis' attorney. "The house needs to be available by the next several months before the . . . "

Both Eva and her lawyer's mouth dropped open at the implication of the statement.

Eva began to wail out loud.

Her lawyer stood and helped Eva to her feet. "I assume that Mr. Reardon's new friend is pregnant then. He'll meet our demands or I'll tie up that brownstone for years."

"Oh God," whispered Eva, being led from the conference room. "He's got a new woman and they're going to have a baby in my house. My house! I painted every room! I installed the tile! I refinished the wood floors!" She yelled, "This just went from bad to the absolute worst. He told me he didn't want any children." Eva grabbed a woman in the hallway. "He said he would love me forever."

"They all say that, dearie. But if they can afford it, they trade us in every ten years or so for a new model. Once the tits start to sag, it's over," replied the stranger in sympathy. "We've all been there. It's just your turn now."

"What happened to true love?" murmured Eva.

Her lawyer snickered. "Surely you don't believe in that crap, do you? Just get the money and run."

"But I do. I do believe in true love," blurted Eva and she cried this mantra all the way home, that night and for the next several days until her body became so dehydrated she couldn't cry anymore.

3

Three months later, Eva signed the divorce papers and slipped them in the stamped mailer as directed. Licking the flap, she closed the mailer with a large sigh. "Well, that's the end of that," she said.

She hurried downstairs so she could catch the mailman whose truck she saw from the window. She caught him coming up the stoop and handed him the mailer.

Giving her a startled look, the mailman grabbed the envelope and hustled down the steps.

"I'm not that bad," she groused, noticing his reluctance to stay and chat.

A mother pushing a stroller hurried by when the toddler saw Eva and started to cry.

"Oh, come on now," complained Eva. Defeated, she pulled back inside the brownstone and looked in the hall mirror. "Jeez." Eva tried to flatten messy hair that would give Medusa a run for her money. Her eyes were sunken, teeth were yellow and dirty, and her skin was sallow.

Her outfit was pajamas that had not left Eva's body for the past two weeks and were straining at the seams as her new diet consisted of chocolate ice cream . . . and then strawberry ice cream . . . and again chocolate ice cream. With chocolate syrup. For a dessert, she inhaled Reddi-wip from the can.

And she stank.

"I'm in some deep, deep doo-doo," lamented Eva looking in the mirror and repelled by what she saw. "You're made of better stuff than this. You're just forty. Only six months ago you were hot stuff." She pulled on her belly fat. "Crap. I'm middle-aged now. The bloom has faded."

She gave the mirror one last pathetic look. "I just can't stop living. This is just a bump in the road." She took another hard look at herself. "Oh, who am I kidding? This is a freakin' firestorm!"

Coming to the realization that she had to battle her depression, Eva climbed the staircase to the third floor. There she took a long shower, washed her hair, shaved her legs and put on some clean underwear. Looking around the bedroom, she found a pair of clean flannel pj's and a tee shirt. To complete the outfit, she slipped on some beat-up flip-flops.

Hungry, she went to the kitchen, but found nothing in the fridge to eat. Frustrated, she began looking for carryout menus when she spotted the airline tickets to Florida.

Eva bit her lip as tears clouded her eyes. "I'm not going to cry," she whispered. "All that is over. I'm going to buck up and get over this. I'm going to get a new life." Staring at the plane tickets, Eva suddenly called her travel agent and ordered a new ticket to be waiting for her at the airport. Then Eva grabbed her coat and purse as she fled the brownstone.

Giving the brownstone one last look, Eva flipped the house key down a street grate.

Dennis would be surprised to discover that Eva had had the locks changed and she had just thrown the only front door key into the New York City sewer system.

Eva felt an immediate sense of relief.

Hailing a cab, she instructed the driver, "JFK please, and step on it."

4

It took only a few hours to fly to Miami.

Eva stepped outside the airport and greedily soaked in the sub-tropical heat. She hailed a cab and got in.

The cab driver didn't seem too happy after getting a good look.

Seeing that the cabbie was dubious, Eva threw a fifty-dollar bill at him.

"Take me to the Fontainebleau Hotel, please," she requested. She had always wanted to stay at the Fontainebleau since it was the hotel used in the James Bond film, *Goldfinger*.

"Are you sure, lady? It costs a lot of money to stay there," he said, eyeing her pajama outfit.

Thankful that she was wearing sunglasses so the driver couldn't see how ridiculous she felt, Eva pulled her coat close about her. "Remember Howard Hughes wore pajamas during the day and he was the richest man in America."

"Really? Never heard of him," the driver replied as he pulled out into the traffic.

"Leonardo DiCaprio played him in a Martin Scorsese movie. You might have seen it."

"Oh yeah. He was that guy who peed in jars and kept them in his room." He glanced in the mirror at Eva.

"You don't do that, do ya lady?"

"Not lately."

"'Cause that is disgusting."

"I would have to agree. You don't have to keep looking back here. I'm not peeing on your seats."

The cabbie shook his head and muttered, "I get all kinds."

"What was that?"

"Nothing, ma'am. Be there soon. You've missed the rush hour."

Eva settled into the back seat and stared out the window.

Unlike New York with its cold gray shadows and dark alleys, Miami was flooded with brilliant sunlight that danced off glass skyscrapers. New York was a concrete jungle, but Miami was the Emerald City. Everywhere were vast expanses of deep turquoise water, white sails, expensive cars zooming here and there and sun-drenched mansions.

Suddenly it was too much for Eva. She felt overpowered by the immense glass city, which resembled a mirror. It made her feel raw inside, too exposed. "Listen," she said, throwing a hundred dollar bill into the front seat. "I've changed my mind. Get me out of here."

"Where you want to go?"

"I'm not sure. All this glass and sun. It's too hectic. I need something calmer."

"The Everglades?"

"God, no! The last thing I need is to encounter an alligator. I just got rid of one reptile in my life."

"Depends on what you're looking for. How about the Keys?"

That was a possibility. Things were slower in the Keys, weren't they? And she didn't know a soul in the Keys. Not a one.

"I just want to rest. Relax."

"Then Key Largo."

"Key Largo," murmured Eva, thinking of the Lauren Bacall and Humphrey Bogart movie. "Yes, take me there."

"Where in Key Largo?"

"Just a nice hotel."

"How nice?"

"A hotel with a nice pool. I like to swim."

"Motel okay?"

"No. I want a hotel. One that will have a concierge."

"You got more money?"

"YES! Just get me to Key Largo." Exhausted, Eva fell back against the seat. "Please, no more talk. Just drive."

Sulking, the driver changed lanes and made his way to Highway 1 heading for the Keys.

Two hours later, the driver stopped in front of an expensive chain hotel. "This okay, lady?"

Eva looked out the car window and nodded. "It will do for now." She paid the driver the exorbitant fare plus a two hundred dollar tip.

He no longer thought Eva was crazy, but merely eccentric. Rich people were never crazy, just different. She would make a great story for his family over dinner. Eva motioned for the hotel valet to open the cab door and help with various packages.

She had stopped at a mall on the way and had purchased some casual outfits. As soon as she stepped out of the cab, the silky breezes of the Keys enveloped her.

Eva took a deep breath.

The salty air smelled like home.

She felt the pain in her broken heart dull a little.

Eva no longer felt that she was going to die.

Perhaps with a little luck, she just might recover . . . even flourish.

Josiah's Songs

Songs that inspired the Josiah Reynolds Mysteries

Bill Monroe - *Blue Moon Of Kentucky*
Joni Mitchell - *Big Yellow Taxi*
The Doors - *People Are Strange*
Pat Benatar - *Wuthering Heights*
Miles Davis - *Kind of Blue*
Big Maybelle - *I Ain't Mad at You*
Julie London - *Cry Me A River*
Maria Callas - *Madame Butterfly*
Merle Haggard - *Sin City Blues*
Dwight Yoakam - *Readin', Rightin', Rt 23*
Joan Sutherland -*Delibes: Lakmé*
Chris Isaak - *Wicked Game*
Johnny Cash - *Hurt*
Jefferson Airplane - *White Rabbit*

WS. 11/16
O 5/17
B 11/17
H 5/18

CPSIA information can be obtained
at www.ICGtesting.com
Printed in the USA
LVOW11s2124311016
511037LV00001B/22/P

9 780615 765556